THE
NIGHT
OF THE
MOTHS

ALSO BY RICCARDO BRUNI

The Lion and the Rose

THE NIGHT OF THE MOTHS

RICCARDO BRUNI

TRANSLATED BY ANNE MILANO APPEL

amazon crossing

Text copyright © 2015 by Riccardo Bruni
Translation copyright © 2017 by Anne Milano Appel
All rights reserved.

Previously published as *La notte delle falene* by Amazon Publishing in Italy in 2015. Translated from Italian by Anne Milano Appel. First published in English by AmazonCrossing in 2017.

Published by AmazonCrossing, Seattle

www.apub.com

Amazon, the Amazon logo, and AmazonCrossing are trademarks of Amazon.com, Inc., or its affiliates.

ISBN-13: 9781542049757
ISBN-10: 154204975X

Cover design by M. S. Corley

Printed in the United States of America

THE
NIGHT
OF THE
MOTHS

PART ONE

IT'S THE FAULT OF THE ONE WHO DIES

One

They say strange things about moths. About how they sometimes enter houses. Superstitions, popular beliefs. But there are few people left, these days, who are familiar with them. So no one thought much about all those moths dancing in the woods on the night the body was found.

It looked like a scene from one of those TV detective shows. People out in the street in their undershirts and slippers, kept at a distance by men in uniform. The flashing blue lights reflected on their faces. Ambulance, firefighters, carabinieri, local police. Everything proceeded slowly. There was no hurry. By that time.

There was the scent of wet grass that you can smell just before dawn. Pine resin. Leaves. Flashlight beams bouncing among the trees. And everyone seemed bent on finding a way to edge nearer to the corpse. It's strange how we feel the need to connect with death. Look at it up close, so we can almost touch it. Like the way we slow down when we see an accident on the road. We pass nearby to try to see as much as possible, even though we know we won't like what we see. And yet we can't help it. We can't look away.

Once, when I was still a child, I saw a body on the beach. It was some guy, I think he was a German tourist vacationing in the area. He'd fallen ill while taking a swim. He was enormous. A friend of mine who worked in the restaurant where the man usually went to eat told me that on that particular day the German had downed a plate of spaghetti with clams, some nice fried calamari, and a liter of chilled white. They said he'd suffered a seizure in the water. He'd asked for it. Clearly.

I was at the beach with my grandmother. The body washed up not far from our umbrella. They'd draped a white sheet over it. Nevertheless, people who had come all that way to enjoy their vacation continued soaking up the sun as if nothing had happened. I remember overhearing a man under a nearby umbrella counting up how much a day's vacation cost him, including a three-bedroom apartment rental. He was persuading his wife to stay at the beach, so they wouldn't be wasting their money. And strange as it was to see children swimming and making sand tracks for their marbles right there in front of the body, along with all those people who went on sunbathing beside it, what was really the most surreal was to witness those who purposely trekked from other parts of the beach just to see it. They approached from opposite sides of the bathhouse. Some even came from as far away as the free beach, where word had already spread. They sauntered over in the bright sunlight, taking their children with them too.

Maybe it makes us feel more alive. Because, at that moment, you might say to yourself, "Damn, it really happens in a flash," but then you realize that it was someone else's moment and you experience a wave of relief. Which is the same reason why someone returning from a funeral will crack a few jokes, feel the need to smile, to make love, to be with others and talk a little, to play with the kids. Because once you've gotten so close to death that you can almost smell it, it's nice to feel alive.

So that night the people who had heard the sirens shriek by had left their houses and found themselves on the street with neighbors, friends, and others who were familiar, since in a town of less than a thousand inhabitants (that's in winter, they all said; in summer the population is much greater), everyone knows one another to some degree.

"They found a dead body," people said.

And, as they said it, they felt chills run up and down their spines. Because death is something dark, a black hole that arouses great fear even when it only brushes you.

"If I heard right, it's a boy," they said.

A drowsy child in someone's arms would rather have stayed home and slept. And, if they'd been going to take a stroll through the night-time street market or have a beer at the Centrale, maybe they would have left him at home. But when you hear that someone has died, it's almost as if the ghost were still hovering around, and no one wants to leave the children alone, or even the dogs for that matter, who had mistaken the unexpected outing for their morning walk and were peeing full blast.

"I heard it's a girl from around here," others said.

And then there's a long-suspended moment. No sound, like a photograph. Enrico's profile outlined by the beam of his VW Beetle's round headlights. Maurizio and Betti entering the woods, approaching, being stopped by a policeman. My brother, sitting next to me, his jeans muddied with damp soil. When this long moment passes, in which nothing seems to stir, like a snapshot left teetering on the brink of an abyss, a whole lot of things will happen. Terrible words will be spoken. Because another person was killed, not far from here. And soon other lives will be swallowed up by the secrets that this night will bring with it.

Because you can't escape secrets. You think you can have secrets, that you can keep them, but in the end they possess you.

"Do they know who she is?" they asked.

And to think that it was such a lovely night, such an important summer. I was twenty-five years old. I had recently graduated, without ever attending a class, and in the fall I was to leave that house, that town, that life made up of things always decided by others, never by me.

That evening I had been to a party with Enrico. A few years older than me, he worked in a prominent architectural studio in Rome. He wanted me to go away with him, at the end of the summer. There had been a time in our relationship when I was sure that things would go exactly that way. But that night I had to tell him something that could change everything.

"It's Giancarlo's daughter," they said.

They always said that. And until I went away, I would never be anything else. That's how it is in small towns where everyone knows everyone else. I, on the other hand, liked losing myself in a crowd, walking among strangers. Just try it in a town where if they see you taking a walk by yourself, they assume you're a bit odd. Some will surely say that's the reason why things went the way they did. Because I was odd. Because people need to console themselves when faced with death. They need to persuade themselves that there is always a reason. Like there was for the German who had eaten too much before going for a swim. People need to convince themselves that, somehow or other, it's always the fault of the one who dies.

"It's Alice," they said.

That's me, Alice.

Two

"But did you have to go on Friday?"

Giulia's voice coming through the earbuds has been asking him that since he left. Enrico had anticipated her reaction, as predictable as the signs streaming by on the sides of the road he's driving along, leaving Rome behind.

"This way it won't interfere with work at the studio," he tells her.

"Yes, but this way it interferes with our Friday night."

"I couldn't put it off. By tomorrow, I'll be back to the Remeres problem."

"That guy again?"

"He's not just some guy. It's an important job."

"And you're spending Saturday on it?"

"I had to console myself somehow, since I can't come to your *apericena* for the girls."

Sky and pavement are the same color. A fine rain triggers the automatic windshield wipers at regular intervals. Enrico is driving with his left arm outstretched, hand on the wheel, and the other leaning on the armrest, fingers touching the gearshift. He left early that morning. Giulia would have liked to come with him, but she could not postpone preparations for the apericena, a strictly girls-only-or-at-most-a-few-gay-friends cocktail party to say good-bye to the old apartment. It is *the* social event of the first transition to fall. In fact, Enrico deliberately chose this day, when she would not be able to come, to return to the town. He had not been back there for ten years. Since that thing happened. Too long to predict what effect it would have on him. Better to go alone.

"Remeres . . . I've never heard of anyone by that name," she says.

Giulia had called him not long after he had left. Enrico had the earbuds ready, cable inserted in the old Nokia. She seems tense. In part because deciding whether to put black olives in the baby octopus soup to be served in the rustic-chic microbowls is a decision that cannot be taken lightly on this of all Friday mornings, and in part because everything that concerns Enrico's past makes her feel excluded, a feeling that she is not used to, and finally because, since she's known him, he has never deviated from the ring road when driving.

He'd told her what happened, long ago. It's not the first thing you tell a person when you go out together, he'd explained. They were sitting in a Mexican cantina having a drink. Enrico had told her everything, while staring at a bowl of guacamole on the table in front of him. It was a little like saying, "You know *Twin Peaks*? I was Laura Palmer's boyfriend." And that was more or less the effect the story had had on her. To wash it down she'd needed the help of a couple of margaritas.

"He's a strange character, Remeres . . ." he says to her as he drives along, looking around.

"And how's the car?"

"Fantastic, it's very comfortable and you can't even hear the engine."

"And the onboard computer?"

"I don't know how it works."

"Didn't you read the manual?"

"I shouldn't have to read it. You had them put this thing in. I just wanted a car radio."

"A *car radio*? How quaint!"

He's never liked driving. And since he stopped going to the town on his vacations, he's no longer had a good reason to leave Rome. But at that time, Civitavecchia was like a transition point. His world began where the autostrada ended. Every time he left Rome behind and exited at the tollgate, entering the Aurelia, he began to feel different. An enjoyable holiday feeling, the kind that upon returning is transformed into that sweet nostalgia in which every summer's end remains captive. But the ongoing construction work for the new highway has changed the landscape, the way time changes people. Too bad.

"Do you think you'll see your old friends again?" Giulia asks.

"I don't know, maybe I'll run into someone. Maurizio for sure."

"Maurizio is the one from the agency?"

"Yeah, that's him."

Enrico feels that strange taste in his mouth that his old friend's name leaves. Talking about him to Giulia is like talking about a character you've seen in a TV series.

He changes his grip on the steering wheel, resting his left arm on the windowsill and running his other hand through his windblown hair.

"I would have liked to meet him. Maybe sometime you can take me there, to the shore."

"We're selling the house, Giulia. Usually when you do something like that, it's because you don't feel like going back."

"If you had a Facebook profile, you could keep in touch."

"Forget Facebook."

"But aren't you curious to know what they do? How they've turned out?"

"I find it hideous."

"You're such a bore."

"Did I tell you about the time a guy stopped me in the supermarket and I couldn't figure out who he was?"

"Yes, lots of times."

"I was convinced he was a friend of my father's. When he started asking me about my high school classmates, I thought he was the father of one of them."

"Instead he was your desk mate."

"Not exactly, he sat a few rows up, but yes, he was a classmate of mine. When I realized it, I felt twenty years older, I spent a shitty evening and decided that I'll tell the next person who stops and asks me, 'Is it you . . . Enrico?' that he's mistaken. Can you do that on Facebook?"

Approaching the border with Tuscany, the Aurelia is reduced to two lanes, like a secondary road. And it's at that moment that Enrico begins to recognize the scenery rushing past him. The Maremma countryside is the first breath of his past to come flooding back. And Enrico is surprised to feel a pleasurable sensation, similar to back then. It is not the effect he had feared. And he barely has time to realize it before catching sight of something in that landscape that punches him right in the gut.

"God, how tedious you'll be when you're an old man," Giulia says.

Enrico sees an emergency turnout to the right. He slows down, puts his blinker on, and pulls off the road. He searches for the hand brake on the new car, a station wagon loaded with accessories that reminds him of a huge coffin on wheels, but that Giulia liked so much. There is no hand brake. But, as he is about to tell Giulia, he remembers that the parking brake in that car is a button next to the steering wheel. He wonders if it will work. He presses it and the button lights up.

"The parking brake, Giulia, when the little light comes on, it's set, right?"

"You press the button, the little light comes on, and you can get out."

"The usual lever wasn't good enough."

"Are you already there?"

"No, I wanted to stop and look at something."

"It's raining."

"It's almost stopped here." That's not true.

Enrico turns toward the back seat and grabs his jacket.

"What do you want to look at?" Giulia asks.

Before getting out he lurches back and forth to see if the parking brake, engaged by a luminous button, really works. The car holds. He drapes his jacket over his head as a shield against the fine drizzle and steps out.

"A tower."

There it is, at the top of a hill. From here you can barely make out its profile. Farther on there's a dirt road that leads there.

"A tower?"

"Yeah, an old ruined tower."

"Sounds spooky."

"In college I did a paper on this tower, a small project to turn it into an apartment."

He was really going to buy it. There was actually a time when that project seemed destined to come to fruition.

"An apartment in a ruined tower?" Giulia's voice now seems more distant.

"One room on each floor."

"I can't picture you there."

Enrico remains standing, looking at the tower.

He smiles.

Three

This morning she seems worse than usual . . . help, someone get me out of here!!!

Chiara sends the message on WhatsApp. She checks the time on the iPhone display. Still five minutes before the alarm clock is set to go off, but she won't need it this morning either. This morning once again her parents' voices, down below in the kitchen, were enough.

She turns over and burrows under the covers. She doesn't feel like barging in on them. She'll go down in five minutes, when her father is out of the house and her mother is there alone, staring at a cup of organic tea.

She's a sad woman. A sadness that is contagious.

"The bank refused me, until I recover, they won't give me any more," her father Maurizio is saying. He's talking about money. He'd like to do something, an important investment, according to him. "It's a golden opportunity that we're missing because of a few bucks."

Chiara looks around. The laptop with the "ANONYMOUS" sticker is closed beside the bed, but the LED is flashing and the fan is on because it's downloading the video of Heath Ledger as the Joker. The poster of *Into the Wild* is hanging behind the door. Every time she sees it, she thinks she wouldn't mind dropping everything to run off with Christopher McCandless, follow him to Alaska, save his life or die with him.

Clothes are scattered on the floor and on Margherita's bed—who maybe, in the end, did the right thing by going off to Coldplay's city. She hasn't heard from her sister for days; before, they always used to talk. There's that photo of them together: it's still there, propped against a stack of books piled precariously beside the desk.

"It's not just a few bucks," she hears her mother, Elizabeth, whom everyone calls Betti, say. "And besides, it doesn't matter, we don't have it. And I won't go back to *her* at this point. I won't go asking her for money."

"Fine then, we'll miss a chance, no problem. After all, what the hell do you care."

"Don't be an asshole."

"Look, the investment was for you, for the girls, for all of us. Fuck. It's an important deal, how can you not . . ."

"Please stop."

Silence. Chiara pictures the scene in the Germano kitchen. Her mother is in her bathrobe, kneeling on a chair, bending over the table. With a teaspoon, she is stirring raw sugar into her cup of organic green tea. Her hair is gathered at her neck, and she's watching the water take on an amber hue as the tea leaves packed into the filter release their essence. Her father is standing. He's wearing a blue or gray suit and a pale-blue or yellow tie that brings out his tanning salon bronze, coffee cup in hand, a pack of Marlboros and an orange or green Bic lighter resting near the sink. The scent of aftershave. Hair cropped short, the little that's left of it. Red-framed glasses that make him look attractive. He checks the clock. He checks his cell phone and slips it into his pocket. He gulps down the coffee. He picks up his heavy jacket, puts it on, and zips it up to the neck. He walks to the door. He stops. Hesitates. He tilts his head slightly to hear what his wife is doing. She hasn't moved, her gaze motionless, focused on her cup of tea. Maybe he should say something to her. His mouth tightens, as he tries to think of what he could say. But he can't think of anything so he picks up his keys and leaves.

The sound of the door slamming is her signal. Chiara gets out of bed. She puts on her terry cloth socks. She goes into the bathroom. She sits on the toilet seat and sets the iPhone on the little bench in front of her. A vibration. She reads the message.

What a drag, Kia!!! Sorry about the shitty situation. Hang in there, later I'll tell you something.

She gets up, flushes the toilet. Now her mother knows she's about to come down to the kitchen and she'll wipe away the tears so Chiara won't have to ask her anything. She looks at herself in the mirror. Long, disheveled hair. Cold water on her face. A deep breath. She goes down to the kitchen. Her mother stands up as soon as she sees her and goes over to give her a kiss on the forehead.

"Good morning, sweetheart."

"Morning, Mom."

"Cheer up, it's Friday." She smiles, but abruptly jerks around. She picks up her cup of steaming organic green tea from the table, turns her back, and covers her face with the sleeve of her bathrobe. Then she turns back. "Should we see a movie tomorrow?"

"No, Mom, I'm going out tomorrow night."

"Going out? With whom?"

"You know who." Chiara opens the cabinet door to get the cereal and fills a bowl.

"No, I don't know."

"With Gibo, Mom." She takes the milk out of the fridge.

"Doesn't that sound like the name of a monkey? Gibo."

"It's not his fault that they named him Giovanbattista."

"Could be, but I don't know which is worse."

14

"Why don't you like him?" She pours the milk into her cereal bowl.

"Because he's twenty-one and you're sixteen."

"And because he's an auto body repairman."

"Don't be silly . . ."

"Oh sure."

"Naturally I don't find him stimulating enough company for you."

"He's nice."

"Sweetie, if only being nice were enough."

"Anyway, he's better than my friends. He's more fun."

"That word. 'Fun.' I'm not all that crazy about it, you know?"

"Why? Don't you want me to have fun?"

"It sounds like something I don't like when my daughter says it."

"You don't like people to have a good time."

"Why do you say that?"

"Because it's not as if anyone has much fun in this house."

Chiara sits down at the table and starts spooning up the cereal.

"And that's my fault, you think?" Betti asks.

"It's not my fault."

"There are three of us."

"He'd love to have fun."

"Oh, perfect."

"It's true."

"Right, it's true. It's all the harpy's fault."

"It's called a *ballbuster*, Mom."

The slap lands hard on the back of her head. The spoon falls out of her hand and ends up in the bowl, splashing the milk. Chiara remains still. She lifts her hair out of the bowl, then straightens up slowly. She stares at her mother.

"Chiara, why do you treat me this way? At one time we used to get along."

"Look what you did." She shakes the milk-soaked cereal out of her hair.

"Go get dressed or you'll be late."

"Now I have to take a shower. Clearly I'm going to be late."

"All right, hurry up and I'll take you."

Chiara gets up without another word. She feels like screaming. Letting her rage explode and hit her mother with the force of a cyclone. But there's Saturday night out with Gibo and his friends at stake. She runs up the stairs. Goes into the bathroom, undresses. She drops everything on the floor and gets into the shower. It will take tons of time to dry her hair. She smooths the body wash on her shoulders, breasts, belly. When she reaches between her legs, she lingers. She stops. She touches herself lightly. A shiver rises up. Gibo's hand was there the other night. At first a little too rough, but then more gently. She'd liked it. She'd like him to do it again.

Touch her like that forever.

"Chia, get a move on." Her mother's voice comes from the hall.

Chiara rinses off. Turns off the water. Slips on the robe.

As she's drying her hair, she thinks that she should cut it. With it long that way, it's too little-girlish.

"How are you doing?" Her again, peeping through the door. She's smiling. She must be over her snit.

"Go away, or I'll be late."

"I'll write you a note. Where's your notebook?"

"Never mind."

"Sure, come on, we'll take our time and get you there for second period."

"I can't."

"Should we have breakfast at the bar? Croissants with jam and a cappuccino?"

Chiara checks the clock. She'll never make it on time by bus. "Okay," she surrenders. "But I want my croissant with pastry cream."

"You know what they use to make that yellow stuff?"

"Mom . . ."

"Okay, I'll wait for you downstairs."

"Good idea."

"But the notebook, where is it?"

"I'll bring it to you."

"Is there something I shouldn't see in that notebook?"

"I'll bring it to you. I have to look through my stuff for it."

"Deal." She's about to close the door.

"Mom."

"What is it?"

"If I see that you've snooped through my things, I'll be pissed."

"Sweetie, 'I'll get angry' more or less expresses the same idea. Save expressions like that for Gibo."

She closes the door.

Chiara grabs the iPhone and taps out a message.

shitty day, the ballbuster made me late 2 bus and is driving me. tell me in class ok?

In a few seconds the balloon appears.

bummer Kia :(:(:(

Four

Enrico is early, by at least an hour. It's stopped raining, but by the color of the sky, you can tell it's only a respite.

Having left the Aurelia, he took the route that cuts through the town, toward the coast road that runs along the shore. He drove slowly, keeping the engine's rpms to a minimum, as though entering his past on tiptoe. He looked around, seeing houses that were familiar, finding them changed, reading the passage of time like on the face of someone you come across after many years. He noted a few passersby, trying to remember if he knew them.

He left the car in a parking lot that now has blue stripes and a parking meter. He took the ticket and read the name of the town printed on it, as if to confirm that he was really back there. After ten years. He covered the distance that separated him from the real-estate agency as though sleepwalking, hoping to find it open. But time around here has a different tempo, and the office was still closed. He turned back. He felt something like a sense of vertigo at finding himself in the midst of those houses, so close to the piazza and to the Centrale.

He thought of returning to the car and driving around.

He glanced toward the Centrale, commanding his nerves to relax.

Then he finds himself at the counter.

There's a girl reading the newspaper. She's wearing a black apron. The bar's decor hasn't changed all that much, and the effect of being back in time knocks the breath out of him.

"Morning," the girl says.

"Good morning," Enrico replies. "Can I get a coffee, please?"

At that moment the door to the storeroom opens and Carletto, the Centrale's manager, enters.

"Pop, where are the *tramezzini*?" the girl asks.

Carletto has put on weight. His hair is grayer, his eyes redder. He seems wearier.

"Get them from the kitchen. I'll handle things here," he says.

Enrico follows his movements. He's surprised to know those gestures by heart, somewhat like rediscovering them. Carletto nods, pursing his lips as if about to kiss the espresso machine as he pumps the coffee into the cup, which he then sets in a saucer on the counter, adding a chocolate and presenting it with a "voilà."

He always says that when he serves the coffee, and that's when you notice the subtle hint of wine on his breath, already so early in the day.

But Enrico does not immediately pick up the coffee. Carletto notices his hesitation. He looks more closely at him. Enrico sees that he is trying to remember who he is.

"No! Enrico?"

"Ciao, Carletto."

"It can't be . . ." A hearty handshake. "What the hell happened to you?"

Enrico tries to say something as he pours the packet of sugar and turns the spoon in the coffee cup. He can't come up with anything, just a sigh that becomes a tight smile, a cry for help.

"How many years has it been?" Carletto asks him.

"Ten."

"Ten years already, *mamma mia*. Around here everything seems the same, just a little quieter. There are fewer people. Remember those evenings, when I had to kick you all out and send you home because you were always here? Mother of God . . . How I miss those times. There were a helluva lot of them. Remember Malarima? That old man came down every night threatening to call the carabinieri. What fits he had! But what about you? What are you up to? Where did you end up? What are you doing here?"

"I came to sell the house."

"Ah, so you're not coming back."

"No, I'm not coming back."

Carletto nods. "Drink your coffee, go on."

He turns away and arranges a few bottles. Then he goes back to the kitchen.

Enrico takes the cup and brings it to a table. He scans a few headlines in the *Gazzetta*. There's the page about Roma training for Sunday's game. On the wall is that Daffy Duck clock. It's another thing he hadn't remembered, but now it's as if it had always been there, in his memory, buried underneath some other items like so many objects stored higgledy-piggledy in a trunk. And he wonders how many times he must have looked at that clock, how many hours he spent waiting. How many minutes he watched slip through those hands, in this bar, with his friends, on one of those many summer days waiting to go to the beach, or having returned from the beach, waiting to decide what to do later that night, or after supper, waiting to get everyone together, until in the end he remains there shooting the breeze rather than doing anything else, and sooner or later someone else shows up, but it's never the one he was waiting for. And as the hands of the clock inch along, robbing seconds from his day, he realizes that everything that is left around him, all of it, every face, every object, every sound, every gesture, every smell, even a breath that reeks of wine early in the morning, is ultimately nothing more than another piece of the same memory, of that face, of her gestures, of her voice, of all the time he spent with her.

Alice.

From the kitchen there is only silence. A telling silence: someone is no doubt whispering, surely saying that the guy out there was her boyfriend. The one she should have been with when she was killed. For sure he's saying that the guy never got over it, that he never came back here, and that now he wants to leave it behind for good. And maybe it's better that way. Because that memory is stuck to him and he drags it along like a shadow that people can't help noticing.

Enrico drinks his coffee. *Totti plays starter.* He carries the cup to the counter. He searches for change in his pocket. He has a two-euro coin. He glances at the kitchen door. Places the coin next to the cup. Before leaving he checks the time on Daffy Duck's hands. He opens the door, the little bell tinkles, nobody comes out, the shadow follows him.

Take care, Carletto.

Out on the street it's cold. It's raining again. There's the smell of salt in the air that the wind picks up on the shore and carries to town.

"Enrico . . ."

He turns. Carletto is at the door to the bar.

"Remember? The first of the season is always on the house," he says, handing back the two-euro coin.

"It's still a long time until the season."

"It means you'll come back and have another coffee."

The barista says good-bye and goes back inside; shutting the door behind him, he immediately resumes his usual activities. His daughter sets the *tramezzini* sandwiches out on the counter and goes back to leafing through the newspaper.

Seen from outside, a bar is not all that different from an aquarium.

Beta Realty is across the street. Enrico spots a young woman running with a newspaper held over her head. She gets to the office, drops her keys on the ground, picks them up, and opens the door.

Five

My last day was August 8. It started out as a radiant morning. A brilliant sun. Midsummer. I would leave that month. The plan was to go and live with Enrico, though maybe everything was about to change with him.

After high school ended, my father, Giancarlo, had asked me to stay because he needed me. My family ran a restaurant. An isolated place, along the provincial road to Carrubo. A renovated old farmhouse. We lived upstairs. Home and business combined. But since things were going well, my father had decided to expand and had started constructing another building that would serve as a hotel. Then he would entrust the new operation to my brother, Sandro, and would give me a hand to do what I wanted. That's what he said, but in reality, what I wanted had never sat well with him.

As it was, he didn't like the fact that I was studying. He didn't like the idea that I wanted to leave. He didn't like Enrico, who wanted to take me to Rome with him. Right now, it was about getting the hotel built, but afterward he would want me to stay to help get the business started, and after that he would say he needed me for a little while longer. At least until the day I decided to stay, having found someone local, gotten pregnant, or something like that. That was their creed. But unlike them I recited a poem by Bukowski every morning: "I am not like other people. / I'd die on their picnic grounds . . ."

Amen.

It was a Tuesday. We were closed today. I had a date with Enrico. He was to arrive that same day from Rome, a little late into the summer, which had happened more and more often since he'd started working at the studio. We'd been together for several years. Sometimes it seemed like we had always been together.

At the beginning, many summers ago, I was head over heels. He was here with his family. All the girls had a crush on him because of those big blue eyes. One day, I was at the beach with my girlfriends, and he came over, told me about a beach party, asked if I wanted to go with him. I knew my brother was going, because that's all he'd talked about for a week, so I figured that maybe I could manage to go too. I said yes. No sooner had he gone than my friends started carrying on, laughing, cheering, teasing me, enough to make you want to bury your head. Anyway, that's how it started.

Enrico came back every summer so we could be together. In the winter he came whenever he could. Sometimes he told his parents that he needed some peace and quiet to prepare for an exam, and then he'd come back for a while and we would spend time together. They were fantastic days, at his house. We listened to music, smoked weed. He told me that he was going to buy an old tower nearby, where we could escape, shutting out the rest of the world. In my father's and my brother's eyes, he was just a typical Roman city boy who came here to find a girl for the summer and have some fun. For them anyone who wasn't born in our town was only good for his money, to pay for his meal and leave a tip. But they were wrong. Enrico was a nice person. And I bet he still is, even though he never did go back and buy that old tower.

Anyway, that day he was supposed to come and pick me up in his yellow Beetle. But my father, who apparently was determined to get in the way, called me on my cell phone and told me to come down, he had something I needed to do for him.

"The shopping, Alice. Sandro is at the gym and I need a few things. I have to stay in the kitchen and make the sauces."

"We're closed today. I'm going into town."

"After you do the shopping."

"But Sandro went to the gym."

"The shopping list is in the kitchen."

It pissed me off whenever that happened. And it happened a lot. *Sandro is at the gym, Sandro is tired because he got home late, Sandro doesn't feel too well* (maybe because Sandro came home plastered, but what do you expect, *he should have a little fun with his friends now and then . . .*). *Anyway, Alice, what else do you have to do?*

I took the list and the keys for the Pandino, and stopped to smoke a cigarette before heading out. If I smoked in the car, it would leave a smell and then they'd get on my back about that. Smoking was another one of those things that Sandro could do, but if I did it, it was suddenly wrong.

So I was smoking when I saw something move behind a bush. I hid the cigarette in the palm of my hand and peered through the leaves. Strange noises. It sounded like a dog panting hotly. I thought it was Drago, Sandro's old German shepherd. I moved aside a branch. And that's when I saw him.

Hidden behind the foliage of the bush was the Half-Wit, who was jerking off as he spied on me. Disgusting. He stared at me with those pale-gray eyes, not even pausing. No way. His mouth was open and a trickle of drool dribbled down onto his shirt. I took a step back. I dropped the cigarette and jumped into the car. I turned the key nervously, and floored the gas pedal while the car was still in neutral. The gear was always a little stiff and the clutch sometimes didn't work well. Anyway, when you hurry things always go wrong. But, as soon as I was able to put it in first, I sped away, keeping an eye on the branch of the bush that kept swinging back and forth in the rearview mirror.

It wasn't the first time it had happened. It wasn't the first time I'd caught the Half-Wit with his pants down and his dick in his hand. If I'd told my father, he would have slaughtered him. And I didn't like my father when he became a raging beast. Like when he lit into the foreign workers at the construction site because they screwed something up. But I'd have to tell Sandro. Because the Half-Wit was starting to scare me.

Six

"I'm sorry about the wait, Mr. Sarti. It's just that strep is making the rounds this year at my son's nursery school." Her name is Carmen, the girl at the agency whom Enrico had spoken to on the phone when he'd called to explain his situation. People's faces never correspond to the image you have of them when you hear their voice first. Carmen's voice is high-pitched, a thin, nasally, unpleasant sound that Enrico had associated with an appearance decidedly different from the woman now before him. Dark complexion, black hair, impenetrable eyes. A slightly sweet and invasive perfume saturates the air inside the agency.

"Don't worry about it," he tells her.

"Excuse me?"

"Being late, don't worry about it."

"Thank you."

Carmen takes a green slip of paper out of the top drawer of the desk, scans it for the codes. She enters them into the computer, tapping the keys with long nails polished a very dark red, the same shade that glosses her lips.

"So then, let's see," she says, scrolling through the information that the computer has brought up. "From what I can see, since we've been managing it, the property has always been rented. It seems it's done well, are you sure you want to sell? Have you considered the fact that in this location a house like yours is always a good investment?"

"I'm moving to a new house, in Rome, and I want to do it all without taking out loans. Then, if I have anything left in my pocket, so much the better. I'm getting married."

"Oh really? Congratulations."

"Thanks."

"And you have no plans to come back on vacation?"

"We haven't come here for quite a while. My parents always preferred the mountains, my sister lives abroad, and I . . ." *I? I what? You see, I used to go with a girl who was killed in this town, but how could you possibly not know that? I thought that as soon as you saw my name, you'd jump out of your chair. Because you know what people say? That it was my fault, that I let Alice go home alone. And I spent the next ten years trying to convince myself that people were wrong, without ever really succeeding. Believe me, coming back here wouldn't be my first choice for a vacation.*

"I think we'll go somewhere else."

"Anyway, the house is in perfect condition, so there won't be any difficulties. It might have been a problem for a lower-end property, but those interested in properties of a certain type are definitely not affected by the housing crisis."

"Let's hope so."

"I've prepared a prospectus for you, with an estimate and some documents to sign to get the whole thing started. In the meantime, I'll take care of the rest. Can you come back next week to finish up?"

"Next week?"

"Yes, that's right. Would Monday work for you?"

"I was hoping to finish up today."

"There's no way I can do it today, sorry," Carmen says, as if it were embarrassingly obvious.

"Maybe tomorrow?"

"Tomorrow is Saturday."

"It's just that I didn't think it would take so long."

"We're part of a network of agencies, Mr. Sarti. The steps are a bit more complicated, but it guarantees a better job and a more rapid conclusion of the matter. Look, if you come back Monday morning, before lunch, I'll have everything ready for you. That way you'll sign and we'll be done. Meanwhile, I'll leave you the keys, maybe you'd like to go see if there's anything you want to take with you, or if there's anything that needs repairing, just anything you'd like included in the paperwork. You could spend one last weekend there, especially since the house isn't rented at the moment."

Carmen retrieves a bunch of keys from a drawer and sets them on the desk in front of him. Enrico recognizes it immediately. The gold key ring with the spring catch is his mother's. Each time he took that set of keys when he left Rome, he already felt better, as though he were escaping.

"It goes without saying that if between now and Monday you were to have second thoughts, there's still time to stop everything without a charge. Later, precisely because of the network, closing the file might incur some agency fees."

"Thank you," Enrico says, staring at the keys and trying to understand why it's so difficult to pick them up. "But I really don't think that will happen."

"I just want to make you aware."

"Isn't there someone who can take care of this?"

"What do you mean?"

"The house, going there to see that everything is in order. Basically you people have been taking care of it."

"Yes, but as I said, at this time it's not rented, and today is Friday."

"Today is Friday, tomorrow is Saturday, and yesterday was Thursday . . . When should I have come?"

Carmen smiles, embarrassed.

"There are set times that . . ."

"Excuse me, but I was hoping to return to Rome."

"I'm sorry."

The bunch of keys, there on the desk.

Betti and Chiara leave the house. It's raining. Betti takes the one umbrella left by the doorway and opens it, and they huddle under it as they run to the car.

They jump in quickly.

"What shitty weather."

"Chiara, darling, would you at least try not to talk like a sailor?"

"Why does everyone have it in for longshoremen?"

"It's a figure of speech."

"I don't think longshoremen are a particularly foul-mouthed category."

"All right, Chiara, then try not to be foul-mouthed, please. I wish you'd see that . . ."

"Mom, that guy is signaling you."

Betti looks out the window. A worker with an orange vest is waving his arms in the air. Betti stops and rolls down the window.

"Not that way, lady, unless you want to go skating."

"Sorry, what are you saying?"

"Didn't you see the sign?"

Betti looks back. In fact, there is a small sign placed on the ground, not far from the gate of their house.

"And you think that sign is visible enough in this weather?"

"That's what they gave us, lady."

"Why, what happened?"

"The usual problem from that oil refinery."

"Oil again?"

"Liters of it, ma'am, and no sign of stopping. With all this rain, things seem to be getting even worse."

"But it's the third time this month. Can't they come up with a solution?"

"Sure, there's a solution. All it takes is for someone to buy the site, with the entire reserve, and drain it. It's sometimes done when they tear down a gas station or something like that."

"Damn it."

It takes Betti a few tries to make a U-turn. The guy with the orange vest helps her maneuver, giving her instructions.

"You'll see, with that sign on the ground like that, sooner or later someone will end up having an accident," Betti calls out the window, heading the opposite way.

The bunch of keys is now resting on the passenger seat.

Enrico is driving slowly down Via delle Ortiche, where the house is. He has the earbuds in again and his phone lying beside the keys.

"What sense would a hotel make? I'll go directly to the house, that way I can check things out, see if there's anything I want to keep. If it turns out I can't stand staying here, I'll come back to Rome, don't worry."

"Your voice is panicky. I don't think it's a good idea." The plan clearly doesn't appeal to Giulia.

The car slows down. Enrico pulls over to the side of the road, beyond which the pine woods extend to the beach. He lowers the rain-slicked window and stares straight ahead. His eyes are nearly squinting in the colorless light that has suddenly become so bright.

The gate of the house is in front of him. Wooden planks alternating with iron bars don't allow you to see beyond it. An engraved snake encircles the keyhole. From the car you can scarcely make it out, but he knows what it is. His mother wanted it there. An ancient Egyptian symbol of protection.

That's the place. The precise spot where he would stop the car each time, step out, and insert the key into the snake's mouth. At that moment, every time, there was already the scent of vacation, of that world that was about to open up.

The key ring now holds a remote-control device as well. Something new: an added convenience for renters who don't have time to waste on old locks and superstition.

He presses the button and the gate opens onto the tree-lined lane.

The Daffy Duck clock is really horrible, Chiara thinks as she squeezes the cream out of the half-eaten croissant, practically sucking it out. With a finger she draws a smile in the foam of her cappuccino.

Carletto's daughter is behind the counter reading a newspaper. Her name is Caterina, and she finished high school last year. Chiara had smoked in the bathroom with her a few times. Caterina had told her about a friend of hers who lives in New York and who had asked her to come stay with her for a while, so they could make the rounds of clubs where they have live music. Jazz or something like that. Now, seeing her behind the counter with an apron on, right under the horrible Daffy Duck clock, it's sad.

"What are you thinking about?" asks Betti. Her mother is holding a cup of wild-berry tea, letting the steam waft up into her nostrils.

"I'm thinking I'd like to be someplace else," Chiara says, observing her smile.

"Where?"

"In London, with Margherita."

"We've discussed that."

"So? She was sixteen when she left, the same age I am now. She's working now and could put me up."

"But you have to finish school."

"I could finish it the way she did."

"Margherita can't support you for two years and we can't afford it."

"Money."

"You say that as if it were a dumb reason."

"If you only listened to him, and asked Grandma . . ."

"What do you mean?"

"You know."

"So, were you eavesdropping on us this morning?"

"Sometimes it's hard not to."

Chiara raises her eyes from her cappuccino and looks straight at her mother.

"All right, I'm sorry. Finish your breakfast and I'll drive you to school."

"Why don't you talk to Grandma anymore?"

"Why do you all only bring up your grandmother when you're talking about money?"

"And you, what do you have against her? She's your mother . . ."

"Drop it, Chia."

"As usual."

"As usual what?"

"As usual, when you don't want to answer, you just claim you're right without ever explaining anything."

"Your grandmother is not the person you think she is." Betti sets her cup on the table. "Your father is convinced that if I asked her for it, she'd give me the money and that's that. It's not that simple. She'd use the money to interfere again, to criticize me, to impose her way of doing things, which . . ."

"Which?"

"Which is the wrong way."

Chiara pushes aside what's left of her croissant to focus on her cappuccino. She takes a sip, then puts the cup down, wiping the milk mustache under her nose with a napkin. She takes a deep breath, then comes out with it.

"I went to see her."

"What?"

"This summer, with Valentina."

"Why did you do that?"

"Because you didn't want me to."

"What a terrific reason, one that makes me so proud of you."

"So what's new: you're never proud of me."

"Sometimes you're so stupid."

"Can we go now?"

"No, we can't go. Not until you tell me why you disobeyed me."

"I felt like going, okay? I don't understand why I haven't been able to see my grandmother, just because you argued with her. So, I took the train and went there with Valentina."

"Oh Lord." Betti closes her eyes and buries her face in her hands.

"Don't you even want to know what she told me?" Chiara asks.

"What did she tell you?"

"That you're a good person and that I should listen to you."

"And?"

"She had a bunch of stories about the family, about you when you were little. She said I look a lot like you."

"And?"

"And she gave me four hundred euros."

"What?"

"To pay for the ticket."

"She lives seventy kilometers from here. Did you go by helicopter?"

"She's never even been able to give me a little pocket money. Maybe it made her happy to give me the money."

"Of course, that way when you ran out you'd go back to see her."

"I didn't go back."

"So what did you do with it?"

"I spent it with Valentina, movies, the pizzeria, reloading my phone minutes that you never do for me."

"Did you buy drugs?"

"What the fuck, Mom?"

"Don't use that language or you'll get it, right here in front of everybody."

"In front of Caterina, you mean."

"In front of whomever. Answer me."

"No, I didn't buy drugs."

"Cigarettes?"

"Those aren't drugs."

"You stink of cigarettes sometimes."

"Gibo smokes."

"Obviously."

"But he doesn't do drugs."

"Oh sure, he's naturally stoned."

"What have you got against him?"

"I told you earlier what I have against him. And don't change the subject, we're not done with the fact that you went to see your grandmother."

"There's nothing more to tell. I told you everything."

"How was she?" Betti loosens up a bit, but still remains on guard.

"She's aged, but she was fine."

Betti drops the spoon in the cup. She pinches the bridge of her nose with her fingers, like when she has a migraine.

"Excuse me, Chiara, I'm going to the ladies' room for a minute."

She's about to cry, Chiara knows it. She always cries, sooner or later. Chiara waits, finishing her cappuccino. She feels like lighting up one of the Marlboros she has in her backpack. Maybe later.

Betti comes out of the bathroom and goes to pay. It's strange to see her talking to Caterina. They seem to belong to two worlds, so far apart, and yet there they are, moored to a five-euro receipt.

"Betti." Carletto, the bar owner, emerges from the kitchen. "You know who was here this morning?"

◆　◆　◆

"Enrico is the guy whose girl was found dead, right?" Chiara asks.

They're back in the car. Betti is driving toward the school. The news that Carletto told her seems to have upset her even more than the news of Chiara visiting her grandmother.

"Yes, do you remember him? We were very close, the two of us."

"Did you sleep with him, Mom?"

"No, what are you talking about?"

She even blushes.

"He was the guy you'd describe as 'my best friend,' the one I told everything to." She has tears in her eyes again. Hopeless.

"So how come you never kept in touch?"

"He went away, and he never came back."

"Because of what happened with that girl?"

"You really don't remember anything about that time?"

"I remember some things," Chiara says, looking out the window at the puddles that have formed along the street. "But nothing definite. Some faces, sure. Who knows if his face is among the ones I remember."

"He came back to sell the house, your father told me. Do you remember the one? We went to see it one day. The one on Via delle Ortiche, with the round swimming pool."

"Yeah, I know, that house is beautiful. I guess money isn't a problem for Enrico."

"It never was for his family. Yet he drove here in that run-down Beetle of his. He wasn't one to put on airs."

"Ask him to dinner."

"To dinner?"

"Usually that's what you do with old friends."

"And what do you know about old friends?"

"It's what I would do."

"Then we'll invite him to dinner. Maybe your father already has."

They arrive at school. Betti signs the excuse in the notebook. Chiara opens the car door. She's about to step out, but stops.

"Mom."

"Sweetheart."

"I'm sorry about the thing with Grandma."

"All right, but promise me one thing."

"I won't go again."

"That's not what I was going to say."

"What then?"

"That if you feel like going back again, next time you'll tell me."

"I promise."

A kiss. Chiara gets out. She feels her mother's eyes on her. Betti watches her walk away, tears still in her eyes. Chiara thinks she can hear her thoughts. Her mother is always moved by how much she has grown. Who knows if it was like that with Margherita. When her sister was born, Betti was very young, just two years older than she is now. Sometimes Chiara thinks about that, and it feels a little strange. Chiara is reminded of that old song that Betti sings to her all the time, the one by that vocalist with the very deep voice who sings those songs that are hard to understand and sometimes even a little dull. There's one that is really beautiful, about Mary, the mother of Jesus. "Girls one day, then mothers forever." And Chiara realizes that she is finally old enough to understand what it means, and why her mother likes it so much.

Chiara turns and sees her mother there, in the car, watching her and waving at her, smiling. She knows she has already forgiven her for everything and imagines her eyes must certainly be teary again, even if she can't tell from here.

Enrico stops the car on the gravel drive and gets out. The house is still partially covered by climbing ivy. Trees, big pots of flowers. The plants haven't been cared for, and there are fallen leaves on the ground. As Carmen told him, the house is not currently rented. The porch, the coffee table with the wicker sofas. Those are different, but they're still in the same place. Enrico approaches, tries to peek inside the house, but the shutters are all closed. He follows the walkway around the house to the other side, where the garden and the round pool are. The pool is empty.

As soon as he opens the door, he's assailed by a musty, stale odor. The furniture is draped in white sheets. He opens the windows to air things out, light filling the room.

The sofas are different: they were once white, but are now covered in a dark-gray fabric. The TV is an HD flat screen, a distant relative of the old cathode model, which used to stand proudly in the middle of the living room.

The bookcase. Enrico remembers that the books only filled two shelves. Now, all four shelves are full. He moves closer. Checks the titles. He doesn't recognize the ones that occupy the two new shelves. He takes one out, a John Grisham thriller that he hasn't read. He opens it and finds an inscription on the first page: "Eleonora and Alfredo, July 2008."

He opens some others. More signatures, more dates. These were books left by renters of the house. Novels read during vacations. Maybe the first tenants left one and the others followed along, thinking it was a household tradition.

At the top, on the left, he recognizes *Exercises in Style* by Raymond Queneau. Alice used to pick it up, open it to a random page, and read whatever she found. She liked the idea that a story could be told in so many different ways.

And in an instant the coal-gray sofa turns white again. The light coming through the windows assumes the intensity of the summer sun. The smell is now the scent of jasmine blossoms that a slight breath of wind carries with it from the garden. Alice is lying there in her bright beach dress, her bare feet propped up on the arm of the couch. She's holding the book.

"Maybe I don't even feel like going to the beach. It will be packed with people today."

"That's what happens in August," Enrico says.

"Let's take a trip."

"A trip? Now? Where would you like to go?"

"To Biarritz."

"What's that?"

"It's a place, in Aquitaine, in the South of France. At one time it was a village of fishermen and whales."

"I don't see you fishing for whales."

"It takes thirteen hours, more or less, to get there. I think it's the closest place to the ocean from where we are right now. Just think: we'll leave, put on some music, and before dawn we'll be at the ocean."

"And what will we do there?"

"Isn't it enough just being at the ocean?"

"It seems senseless to me . . ."

A sound. And it all vanishes. The sofa is gray again. Enrico glances at the window. He walks over to it. Something is moving in the bushes, near the gate. A black jacket, possibly. There is someone out there who doesn't want to be seen.

Enrico rushes to the door, opens it. He looks in that direction, but doesn't see anything. He runs to the gate. He passes the car and checks to see that the bags haven't been stolen. A quick look, but everything seems to be there. The gate was left open. He hears the thud of a car door closing, an engine starting up, and tires screeching like in a detective film. He doesn't see anything. When he gets to the street, he hears a noise in the distance, but the car has already turned the corner. He leans against the gate to catch his breath.

Who was that?

Enrico notices the damaged bush. Snapped branches. The intruder came through there. He makes out a faint path, follows it until he ends up behind a tree. From where he now stands, the front door, his car, and, through the open window, even the inside of the house can easily be seen. He looks around, searching for an explanation or, at best, a clue. But he doesn't find anything. For now he has to settle for the certainty that someone broke into his garden and probably stopped to spy on him.

"You have to report it to the police." Giulia's voice is agitated, and Enrico realizes right away that he should have kept it to himself. That's one of those things you always realize too late, when it should have been obvious. But Giulia's umpteenth phone call had come unexpectedly, while Enrico was still out of breath, and his mind was not yet focused enough to find a solution to the dilemma of black olives in the octopus soup.

"Forget it," he says, regaining control. "My experience with the police around here hasn't been pleasant."

"Yes, but he could be dangerous. Maybe he's a thief, the kind who empties out second homes. Maybe he was casing the place to come back at night."

"What do you know about thieves casing houses?"

"I've heard about it."

"Where?"

"The other day, at the gym. Some girl on the treadmill was talking about it."

"Okay, Giulia, anyhow, the thief saw that this house was occupied and left."

"I'm worried."

"You caught me unprepared. If you had called me ten minutes later, when I'd cooled down, I wouldn't have even told you about it."

"I was wrong to call you?"

"I didn't say that."

"And are there other things that, with a cool head, you haven't told me?"

"Oh God, Giulia, what kind of things?"

"I don't know."

"There's nothing. You have to understand that coming back here is having a strange effect on me."

"You should have come home and gone back there Monday. Couldn't they have sent you the documents by e-mail? They must have Internet there, don't they?"

"Everything's fine, try to calm down. And forget the olives: I wouldn't put them in the baby octopus soup, because not everybody likes them."

"There's a thief spying on you. I don't give a damn about olives in the octopus soup. I'm calling everybody. I'll postpone the party and come join you."

"Don't call anybody. Have the party, you'll have a good time."

"Okay, but you'll tell me everything, right? Even with a cool head."

"Of course, Giulia. Everything. Don't worry."

"You won't leave out the tiniest detail."

"I won't leave out the tiniest detail, I promise."

"Don't bullshit me. I don't like it that you're there alone and you know it."

"I remembered it smaller, you know?" Enrico changes the subject.

"The house?"

"Yeah, everything. It's strange, isn't it? Usually it should be the opposite."

"Usually."

"Anyway, I don't think you would like it."

"Why do you say that?"

"Too much vegetation, too many trees, and too many bugs."

"I would have loved to have seen it, though." Giulia always drops that hint of resentment with a nonchalance that reminds Enrico of an attacking midfielder who, while looking the other way, kicks the ball with his heel and sends it to the exact spot he intended.

"Yes, but . . ." he tries to respond.

"Sorry, I have an incoming call. It's Erika. It must be about the apericena."

"Okay, say hello for me."

"If you want, I can put her on hold and we can keep talking about the house . . ."

"No, no problem, go ahead and take it."

"*Muaaa*, then."

"*Muaaa*."

They hang up and Enrico goes back to removing the sheets from the furniture. He opens the rest of the windows. In the kitchen, the bedrooms, the study. Alice's image is everywhere. He feels her beside him. Part of that world that he is slowly bringing back to life. Those memories, like books arranged in a second row, behind other books, are all still there. And everything seems to fall back in place, naturally.

Enrico enters his old room. Many things have disappeared. The agency removed them, because it received a clear directive to rent the house. He runs his hand lightly over the desk. Opens the closet. The figurines of the Roma players are gone. The *Blade Runner* poster is gone.

A sound, again.

This time, it's a car, crawling up the gravel drive. Enrico goes to the window. A gray station wagon comes to a stop behind his car.

A man gets out.

Maurizio.

Seven

The Half-Wit's name was Mario Giannetti. He was a short, hefty guy. He had incredible strength and a worm-eaten brain, rotten, in fact. He always wore a light-blue cap to protect his bald head from the sun. My father had hired him as a bricklayer and had put him up in a little cabin in the woods, a kind of shed for tools and equipment. I don't know what charitable instinct made him do it. He said the guy was someone from our town. And, in fact, the Half-Wit's coffee and Montenegro were always covered at the bar. There was always someone there willing to play a game of cards with him, although for him the object of the game seemed to be to slam the cards on the table as hard as possible. He wasn't a violent person, but all that strength and a brain that didn't work right had always unsettled me. Even before I discovered his perversions.

In the end, the obligatory stop at the supermarket—to do the grocery shopping that no one else could be bothered to do—had at least given me the chance to be alone for a while and think about how to handle the matter. After spending some time, more than necessary, among the shelves and freezer cases to calm down, I loaded the shopping bags into the Panda and headed back home, nibbling from a bag of Fonzies as I drove.

I looked around as I stepped out of the car. The Half-Wit was nowhere to be seen.

In the house, I set the bags down on the kitchen counter and began putting the groceries away. When I finished, I checked the time: it was already past ten. Enrico might be awake. I called him.

"Are you up?" I said as soon as he answered.

"More or less."

"Your voice doesn't sound like someone who was working."

"Show a little mercy."

"That's it?"

"Croissant and *cappuccio* ready when I get there?"

"That stuff is against the law at this hour."

"Okay. I'll pull myself together. We'll take a walk, then have a drink with the others before going to the beach?" he suggested.

"The beach? God, it will be so hot . . . Maybe toward evening."

"So we'll stay at my place then, my parents aren't here."

"But didn't you bring along some work?"

"I also brought a supply of DVDs. We'll settle in here, air-conditioning, beer, and chips. It's your day off."

"That's right, *mine*."

"I can't just leave you by yourself."

"A gentleman like you . . ."

"I even have *The Great Gatsby*."

"You really thought of everything."

"I'll come by in about an hour."

"In an hour, I might change my mind."

"Forty minutes."

"If you're not here in half an hour, I'm leaving you."

The owner of the studio where Enrico worked was an architect friend of his mother's, so it wasn't quite the tough internship he liked to talk about so much. He didn't do it to put on airs, he just had no idea what the world was like for other people. It was as if for him things would never change, as if things would stay that perfect forever. And I know I should have told him sooner about the thing I'd been carrying inside me, give him time to understand, but I couldn't bear the idea of shattering that bright, perfect world of his. It wasn't laziness that made him take everything for granted: his horizon really ended in that picture of us on the couch, watching television and eating potato chips. And not because he was naïve, mind you, but because the world he belonged to, that beautiful world in which your employer is a friend of your mother's who showers you with money without expecting anything in return, in which at any moment you can drop everything and retreat to the vacation house with the swimming pool and garden to enjoy evenings with friends, in which you can take off for a week in Paris because you want to see places that will inspire you (I swear, he did that) for a project that perhaps they might assign you in the future. That world, in short, makes you feel so secure that in the end you're apt to forget that it is not the world in which everyone else lives.

"Where's my ACE?"

The fridge door opened, the sound of things I'd just arranged being moved around any old way. It was my brother, Alessandro, who my father always said was strong and handsome like a Greek hero. It was okay when Sandro was still a child, but as time passed, the Greek hero thing (who, technically, was Macedonian) began to be embarrassing even for him, though he seriously believed it.

That morning, just back from the gym, he assumed as always that someone had bought him his orange-carrot juice. Which, out of spite, I had not.

"So where is it?"

"I don't know. Did you buy it?" I asked.

"Didn't you go and do the shopping?"

"For the restaurant, not for you."

He closed the fridge door. Black close-fitting T-shirt to show off his deltoids and biceps. Bleached hair and soul patch.

"Come on, Ali, you know I always drink it."

"And you never buy it."

"In a funk, little sister?"

"A little."

"Where does it hurt?"

"Where it always does."

"Let's see if I can help."

He lifted me off the ground and started tickling me. He'd been doing it since we were kids, to make me laugh. It was as if seeing me laugh reassured him, even when it was just an involuntary reflex. Then he took the cigarettes, lit one, looked around, and offered me the pack.

"Why is the Half-Wit always hanging around?" I asked without taking a cigarette.

"Where should he be?"

"Why here?"

"Because he's loony, because no one else would have him. He's from our town after all. It's a humanitarian thing, in a way. Why?"

"I don't like him."

"I think he's enchanting."

"Idiot."

"Just your type."

"Don't say that, okay?"

"You two have a secret thing going on?"

"I told you to stop."

"What's your problem today?"

"I don't like that guy, get it? He upsets me. He scares me."

"Did he do something to you?"

"He watches me."

"So let him watch, girls like to be looked at."

"You're a moron, Sandro. You don't understand a thing."

"Then explain it to me."

"He was watching me with his dick in his hand, now do you get it?"

"Seriously? Shit."

"You finally got it."

Sandro took a deep drag on his cigarette. He stared at me for a moment, and I had the distinct feeling that he was thinking about what would happen if our father were to find out about it. He tapped the ashes into the sink as if to shake the thought from his mind.

"What a piece of shit," he said.

"Yeah, but don't tell anyone, okay?"

"I'll take care of it. Don't you worry."

"Fine, but don't blow your top. Don't hurt him. Otherwise, all hell will break loose and I don't want that. I'm ashamed, all right?"

"Okay, okay. I told you not to worry."

"What are you going to do?"

"I'll tell him to keep away."

"Will you really do that?"

"Sure, but my throat is too dry to speak, you know. I don't have my ACE juice."

"Don't be a jerk. Will you talk to him today?"

"I'll go over right away, okay?"

"Thanks."

"Shit, that bastard jerked off in front of my baby sister. I can't believe it," he muttered, heading out the door toward the building site.

Eight

Enrico follows Maurizio with his eyes as he gets out of the car and walks up to the door. He's carrying a big box and a paper bag. He rings the bell and checks his watch. Enrico comes downstairs. He turns the doorknob. Ten years disappear in the time it takes to open the door. There he is, Maurizio, his old friend, standing in front of him. He's put on some weight and lost a little hair, but he has the well-kept appearance of a devoted fitness club member.

"What the hell happened to you? Look at the shape you're in," Maurizio says.

Enrico is disoriented, but only for a moment.

His old friend bursts out laughing. "You were speechless. You should have seen yourself! You haven't changed at all."

"You haven't changed either, still the same asshole."

"Ya think?"

"Just a little more tanned."

"A little time at the gym, under the lamp, otherwise you can forget seeing pussy anymore."

"Come on, come in and put down that stuff."

Maurizio is familiar with the house. He's the one who's been taking care of it these past years for the agency. He sets the box and the bag down on the coffee table in the living room and turns to Enrico again. They hug each other.

"Ten years, Erri. Hard to believe."

"Yeah . . ."

When they break apart, there is a moment of silence.

"These are the things I was telling you about," Maurizio says, pointing to the box on the table. "The ones that were left here in the house. I wanted to tell you right away. You would have figured it out anyway and you would have gone on staring at the box. So now we can put it out of our mind. I'll leave it all here for you. You can decide what to do with it. Now we'll deal with this." He picks up the paper bag. "I guess as usual there's nothing to eat in this house. Am I right?"

Enrico realizes what he's pulling out of the bag. He smiles as Maurizio produces two cans of tuna, a jar of mayonnaise, a packet of pitted olives, two focaccias, and two cans of Coke.

"How many of these must we have eaten?" Maurizio wonders.

"Thousands."

"Scrounge up a knife, so we can have some lunch."

A few minutes later, they're sitting in the garden beside the empty pool, focaccia sandwiches in hand. For a moment, it is as if those ten years had never existed, that everything had just aged overnight. Like that science fiction story in *Urania* that Enrico read some years ago, about a guy who undergoes an experiment in order to see the future, but all he's able to see is the present grown old. The people in front of him, the places they're in. It's as if Maurizio were holding the same focaccia from ten years ago, in the same position as then. And yet everything is different, older. Around them, even the garden seems to belong to another time.

"You've decided, Carmen told me. You're selling it all."

"Right, I want to buy a house in Rome, a bigger house."

"Yeah, she told me. Too bad."

"Why?" Enrico is curious.

"Because I always figured that one day you'd come back and we'd hang out here again, like now. But not to end it all."

"You thought I'd come back?"

"Why not? This was a little like home to you."

"Not 'a little,' it was my house, period."

"And you never thought, even for a moment, that . . ."

"You know how it was."

Maurizio takes a bite of the sandwich. He looks around, squinting his eyes.

"A lot of times I thought of calling you," Enrico says, "of talking to Betti, of coming back here. But I would always have been Alice's boyfriend. People would have looked at me and thought about her. You should have seen Carletto's face today as soon as he recognized me. The same expression that even you have. You come bearing focaccias and Cokes, yet within ten minutes here we are talking about Alice. Why would I come back?"

Maurizio wipes his mouth with the paper napkin. He lights a cigarette. Blows out the smoke. He offers the pack to Enrico, but he refuses with a shake of his head and a faint smile.

"And the girls, how old are they?" Enrico asks.

Maurizio smiles at the change of subject. "Margherita is twenty-six, a grown woman. We hardly ever see her. She's in London. Chiara is sixteen. And she can't wait to join her sister."

"I can picture Betti. How is she?"

"Betti . . . is still Betti."

"And the others?"

"Some have left, some are still here. But you know how it is, at some point you lose touch. You feel less and less like going out. Maybe in December we'll go to Egypt with Marco and Valeria, remember them?"

"They're together?"

"Yeah, they started going together a few years after you left."

"But wasn't she going with . . ."

49

"Andrea."

"Right, the surfer."

"One night Valeria caught him with a Brazilian who arrived in town with two kids. And shit, you won't believe it, but they were both his kids. Andrea's. Apparently every time he told her he was going to Brazil to go surfing, he was riding more than the waves."

"And how did it end up?"

"It ended with them getting married, him and the Brazilian, and now they run a beach establishment nearby. Obviously with a surfing school attached."

Enrico tries to sort things out. To rearrange his memories. Maurizio gives him time, watching him, before finally asking, "How did you find the house?"

Enrico knows that the question is just a way to see how he's feeling.

"Okay, eventful."

"Eventful?"

"There was a thief here earlier."

"A thief?"

"I think so, somebody who was watching me."

"That's odd, the area is patrolled. I can tell the security guard to make a few extra rounds."

"Maybe it isn't important."

"Are you sure? You don't want me to notify the police?"

"Is that marshal still there . . . What was his name?" Enrico narrows his eyes, trying to come up with it.

"Torrese," Maurizio tells him.

"Yeah, him."

"Bad memories, huh? But no, he's been gone for some time. But, if you need me to, I'll tell the security service. After all, we pay them, and since we pay quite a bundle, they take us seriously."

"Never mind."

"Whatever you say."

Enrico takes a breath. Holds it. Then takes the leap.

"Giancarlo is dead, right?"

Maurizio sets the Coke down on the table. He nods, as though he's been expecting the question. "Yeah, he died a few years ago. While he was in prison. Something sudden."

"I'm sorry."

"Don't blame yourself for that too."

"It took me ten years to come back here. We might as well talk about it at this point. The thing is I thought a lot about him. About what he did. It's strange, you know, but in the end, I think he was the only one to do exactly what was expected of him."

"He wasn't a good person, you know that."

"The Half-Wit killed Alice, his daughter. He was still holding her necklace when he found him. It must have happened a short time before. It may seem absurd to you, but sometimes I think I understand what Giancarlo was feeling when he killed him."

"Has there been even one day when you haven't thought about that night?"

Enrico doesn't answer right away. Yet the answer is there. It's as if he needed to embrace it before setting it out in the space between them. "No."

Maurizio waits. He gives him breathing room.

Enrico stares at a point in the hedge and continues, "When I got there that night, to the place where they'd found Alice's body, I saw Sandro. I could feel the hate he directed at me. Maybe I even wanted him to pounce on me. Beat me to death. I wanted him to extinguish the pain I felt inside. Help me spit it out. Maybe he would have killed me. Done to me what his father did to the Half-Wit. I read in the newspaper that when they put him in the body bag to take him away, he no longer had a face. That face. At times I think I can see it. At the instant Alice gets out of the car, furious. She slams the door behind her. She bangs it as hard as she can. I reach out my hand. I'm about to get out, to persuade her to come back inside. I'm about to, but I see her reflected in the rearview mirror, stalking off. I am about to, but I don't do it. I don't know why. That's the moment. There are no others that mattered as much. For Alice, for me, for everyone. And it's at that moment that I have the impression I can see it, that face. The Half-Wit. It's as if he were shrouded in darkness. In the woods. He looks at me. He smiles. His eyes narrow when he senses my hesitation. When he realizes that I will not open the door, he knows that Alice is his. And that's the face that I can't get out of my head. That pasty, morbid, obsessed, brutish face staring at me and relishing my weakness. He stands there. Motionless. Waiting for Alice. And I'm the one who drove her to him."

The cell phone rings on the coffee table inside. Enrico turns toward the sound, pulled back from a long journey into the past. He gets up as Maurizio lights another cigarette.

Enrico picks up the phone. A text.

The octopus will have olives. If those bitches don't like olives, they can eat something else. They've stressed me out. XXX.

Nine

The sound of Enrico's yellow Beetle was unmistakable, announcing its approach even before it appeared around the curve.

Enrico stepped out of the car. Jeans and shirt, disheveled hair, a few days' growth of beard. He raised an arm to wave to my father, some distance away, as he came toward me.

"Enrico, dear, how are you?" The voice of my mother, Luciana, reached us from the terrace where she was lying in the sun with a glass in her hand. Usually she put a little peach juice in it to give it some color and disguise the prosecco or, on more inspired days, the vodka.

"Morning, Luciana."

"Have you seen the construction? What do you think of it?"

"It will be a fantastic place."

I said good-bye to my mother and got in the car. We pulled out of the driveway, but the moment the car started heading down to the road, I saw Sandro walking toward my father and behind him, half hidden by a bush, the Half-Wit. He had spoken to him.

My father, Giancarlo Bastiani. He was standing among the workers, explaining what they had to do. He only had to have the surveyor sign some papers. My father always pretended to be busy when Enrico came to pick me up, because he didn't like him. He didn't want him to take me away. For him it was unthinkable that with all the guys around here, I would choose an outsider. At first he said that I was too young, then he said that Enrico was too old, then that Enrico wasn't suitable, that with his kind you never knew what to expect. And then he started in with his *Why do you want to leave, don't you see how beautiful this place is?* and on and on.

"Did you have breakfast?" Enrico asked me.

"I've been up since seven."

"How come?"

"Because the workers get here early."

"The workers show up at seven?"

"Giancarlo always has to ask for more."

"And people don't say no to Giancarlo."

That was a subject he liked. Enrico joked around a bit about my father. Guys do that. It's as if a kind of competition had been triggered between them.

"You're still wearing that thing around your neck?" Enrico asked, pointing to my pendant, a small plastic turtle found in a Kinder egg a few months earlier. Without thinking, I had started fiddling with it, to give myself time. There was that thing I had to tell him, and maybe it would be better to tell him right away. Find a way to start, like, *Can you pull over somewhere before we go to the bar? I have to talk to you.*

"This is Mr. Toby," I said.

"Are you serious?"

"You know the fable of the frog and the turtle?"

"No."

"It's an ancient Chinese fairy tale."

"I'm listening."

"The frog was happy living in her pond and boasted about it. Then one day the turtle described to her how deep and vast the Eastern Sea was. So the frog became sad."

"That's it?"

"It's a kind of warning."

"A warning?"

"That you can be happy with what you have only if you're unaware of all the rest."

"But not everyone is made for the sea."

"That may be, but as I see it, it's the idea of home that fools us."

"The idea of home?"

"The need to have one."

"I'm an architect. I make my living on that need."

"You're from a rich family, that's what you live on. Besides, wouldn't you like having your home always with you? Take just a few things with you, not needing anything more, and go?"

"Go where?"

"That's the point, there's no need for a 'where' to go. You don't need a specific place, when you have everything you need with you, like a turtle in the Eastern Sea."

"Now I get what you mean."

"Seriously? I barely get it myself . . ."

"They're called campers, and I hate them."

I had to laugh—but only briefly, because I had that thing to tell him, that would maybe change everything.

I was so close to letting it all out, but it's like when you search for words and come up with them too late. I missed my moment. We got to the bar without another word.

As usual Enrico left the car in the middle of the street.

All the others were there. We were a big group, like groups on vacation always are. We filled the outdoor tables at the Centrale as if it were a second home. Carletto would give you a discount on the service, but you had to pick up your glass at the counter, which was one way to save on the peanuts and pretzels and not hire waiters for the tables.

When you're part of one of those groups, it seems that winter doesn't exist, because you have the feeling you've gone from one summer to another. Every discussion, interrupted the year before, picks up where it left off, and the months that have passed in the meantime are summed up as *nothing much, just the usual*. For me, however, the winter had existed. It had left a deep rift that I could no longer carry inside me.

Today I'm confiscating the Settimana enigmistica, *no crosswords, you're playing beach volleyball . . . What, you're still wearing those worn-out Filas, you know there are flip-flops with the Brazilian flag that are more stylish . . . Carletto, some ice at least, I'm not asking for an olive but at least some ice . . . I got a new scooter but I always go at the same speed as before . . . And I think I screwed up, but we can also go for pizza, come on, and maybe go to the movies early and then go for a drink on the waterfront . . . Yeah, but see, at IKEA they have air-conditioning, and if you go at this time, there won't be anybody there, and you won't even have to stand in line for the meatballs . . . Yeah, but you don't have midfielders, it's useless to go play at the ends, put in the forward and let him make the kick . . . Did you see that? . . . I disconnected the account because I was hooked and I played even at work, so I just said enough because it was a mess . . . Whatever you think, but if we vote again tomorrow, the same guy will win because this is a shitty country . . . No, no series, I want a film that begins and ends because if I have to wait a week to see what happens, I'm already pissed . . . I tried to read it but after about fifty pages it really didn't grab me and I put it down . . . With fish you need garlic . . . Look, beer is healthier than that colored stuff . . .*

"Alice!" Betti called to her. "Tonight my mother is watching the babies so we can have a little supper at our place." The babies—we all called them that. They were inside, at a little table. Chiara, notebook open and a box of colored markers scattered on the table, and Margherita, earbuds and sunglasses. They were beautiful. Chiara, a little girl. Margherita, already something else. The bored pout of a sixteen-year-old, a skimpy little dress that left her legs uncovered, sandals unstrapped, and a bare foot moving in time to music that only she could hear. "I think Maurizio was going to tell Enrico," Betti said.

"We'll sit out in the garden for a bit, cold pasta and cold cuts, though, because since the girls are with their grandmother, I want to relax."

Enrico and Betti had known each other forever. As children they went to the same beach club in the summer, and in winter they wrote each other long letters that Enrico still kept in a shoebox that a pair of Nike soccer pros came in.

Betti had had her first daughter when she was barely of age. Enrico told me that he had gone to sit in on her final school exam and there she was in front of the teachers, with her big belly, talking about Euripides's *Medea*.

"Shall we go to their place?" Enrico came over with two glasses of prosecco and handed me one.

"Do you want to go?"

"Why? Don't you feel like it?"

"Sure, of course."

"Is something bothering you?"

"No, it's just so hot."

"Come on, we'll take a little drive and then go home."

He turned to finish a conversation he'd started with some guy, about soccer, Roma, the attackers, the transfer market, and all the rest. I didn't want to be alone at that moment. In part because I had that thing inside me that was becoming heavier by the minute. In part because looking at Enrico and forcing myself to smile at him as he talked about Totti, they weren't his eyes I felt on me. They were other eyes. The ones I had fallen into by mistake. The mistake that Enrico had to know about, that would maybe change everything. And I felt those eyes because he was there, among the others, a short distance away from me. And I was afraid that if I caught them, I wouldn't be able to pretend that nothing had happened. Fortunately, I saw Sandro ride up on his motorbike and I managed to take a breath. Usually my brother hung around with another group, but he knew all my friends too. He climbed off the bike. Black T-shirt, taut muscles, Ray-Ban Aviators, his helmet unfastened.

He first went to greet Enrico, with his gladiator version of a handshake, then he came over to me.

We walked a few steps away.

"I talked to him," he said.

"What did you tell him?"

"That if he tries it again, I'll break his legs. And he knows I mean it."

"Did you tell Dad?"

"No, forget that. I'll take care of it. It's better that way."

"Okay but . . ."

"Ali, the Half-Wit is a doofus, he may jack off but he's never touched anyone. Dad keeps him on for that reason. You're thinking of all those movies about maniacs, the monster who lives in the little cabin in the woods and all that. I told him to leave you alone. If he comes around again, tell me and I'll deal with him." He glanced over at Enrico. "And the architect? What's he up to?"

"Talking about Roma."

"*Maggica Roma*, huh?"

Then he made that tough-guy gesture that he liked so much. He kissed the tip of his index finger and placed it on my cheek.

He was leaving when I heard a noise. I leaned around the corner of the bar, toward the back of the place, where the entrance to the outdoor toilets was. A door had slammed. I wondered who it was, if whoever it was had heard what my brother said to me. I didn't want others to know about that thing. I looked around, trying to figure it out. But I gave up, because I really couldn't afford to think about anything else. I had to talk to Enrico, tell him what had happened.

I made a move to go back to him, but another voice stopped me.

"Are you coming tonight?" Maurizio was there, glass in hand.

"Yeah, we'll be there."

"Listen . . ."

"Don't say anything."

"Did you tell him?"

"Not yet."

"Maybe you shouldn't do it."

"We made a decision."

"And you think it's the right one?"

"I think so, yes."

"I don't." Maurizio was agitated.

"I'm sorry," I said.

"I want to talk about it."

"We've already talked about it."

"Alice, you can't just do whatever the hell you want."

"That's enough now, we're here in front of everybody."

"I don't give a damn."

"Your daughters are over there, for Christ's sake."

Betti had gone into the bar, to her daughters. For a moment I had the impression that she had turned toward us. Just then Betti's mother, Steely Gloria, pulled up in her red Alfa Romeo, one of the few things she had saved from her husband, Alfredo, who'd died of a heart attack when he wasn't yet fifty. Maurizio said that had been the only way the man could spare himself a life spent with that woman. He didn't exactly have a good relationship with his mother-in-law. On one occasion, Gloria had even offered him money to go away and leave her daughter alone. Maurizio had told me about it one night when we were together. One of those nights when I was everything to him, when he would have done anything for me, when he couldn't take the life he had any longer.

The girls jumped at the beep of the horn. Chiara ran to her grandmother's car. Margherita grabbed the backpack and followed her sister at a more listless pace. Betti stood there watching them as they climbed into the Alfa.

"If you tell him, all hell will break loose," Maurizio said.

"We should have thought of that sooner."

Ten

Maurizio leaves the cardboard box on the table. He says Betti would be pleased to see her old friend again. He invites Enrico to come to dinner at their house and suggests that it would be best if they were able to keep certain ghosts at bay. Enrico accepts, and soon after he finds himself alone in the house that was never big enough for him to hide from the memories it held.

He sits at the table, the box in front of him.

After what had happened that night, the officer had asked him to stay at the house for a few days, to be available. The police arrived in the evening.

Marshal Torrese said that for the purposes of the investigation, he would have to check the car Alice had been in before she was killed. He had a ruthless look, which turned to satisfaction, when he found the bag of marijuana that Enrico had left in the Beetle's glove compartment after the party at his friends' home. They took him down to the police station and left him in a room. No window. A table and two chairs. Enrico sat on one and, after a few hours, the marshal entered and sat down on the other one.

"For heaven's sake, Sarti, personal use, no problem at all," Torrese began. "But I have to ask. First of all, whether you possess any more, if you maybe planned to sell it here in town, because you wouldn't be the first, if you follow me, to come and have a nice little vacation with some weed so you could score some extra money. And here's where it becomes all the more complicated, my dear young man, because there are two homicides involved. Don't get me wrong, maybe it has nothing to do with them. But if I were you, I would start talking. Tell me where you bought the stuff, for instance. Because I'll let you in on a little secret, Marshal Torrese is an old hand at this job. He's dealt with quite a few little clowns who tried to bullshit him. And when Marshal Torrese's nose itches, there's always some reason for it. It's experience, my dear young man. Hell, maybe you'd been smoking, you argued with your girlfriend because she didn't approve, she got out of the car, you chased after her, you fought, and, just like that, without even intending to but only because you were high, you did something you didn't even mean to do."

Enrico did not say a word. He was waiting for the officer to whom he had repeated his request for a lawyer.

"And don't be an asshole, because I have a cell waiting with three Moroccans who can't stand pretty boys who kill women."

Torrese stood up and straightened his uniform. He smoothed down his hair, sculpted into something slick and shiny. He walked around behind Enrico. The pain was sudden. Enrico saw the trail of blood on the desk as soon as he opened his eyes. Torrese had grabbed him by the hair and slammed his head on the table.

"Hey, boyo, not slumping, are we? Easy now, don't tell me you're already done? Look, the night is long, so you'd better get over it, otherwise you can get hurt in here." Torrese came within a millimeter of his face. His breath was a fetid whiff of garlic and meat being fully digested. "You get me, pretty boy? You might get hurt in here."

The memory provokes a sense of vertigo. Enrico gets up and goes to look for something to drink. Some cold water. He puts a glass under the faucet. He drinks avidly, splashing his shirt. He'd barely made it out of that room, out of that night.

He'd really ticked Torrese off for some reason. But the judge closed the investigation quickly, and the marshal had to have him taken back home. Enrico stayed just long enough to throw whatever he found at hand in a suitcase. He'd been in shock and had moved like an automaton. He grabbed the computer and a collection of things that made no sense, half a bottle of milk, his toothbrush. The cell phone was charging. There were missed calls and messages that he didn't want to read. He left it there. He took the car keys and drove off. Along the way, he stopped at an emergency turnout, and there he finally gave in to the despair he was entitled to. He remained alone for hours. He'd seen how they looked at him. And he needed to convince himself that it had not been his fault.

No one looked after the beach house after that. Then one day Enrico had called the agency and asked Maurizio to go check on the place and empty the pool.

"There are some things of yours. What should I do with them?"

"Hang on to them, one of these days I'll come and get them."

That day had never come. Instead he received a proposal to rent the house: Maurizio would see to it himself. A few documents by registered mail, and that was it.

The box, on the table.

Enrico goes over, sits down again. He inhales. Exhales.

Opens it.

A couple of tees, a few shirts, and some jeans. A bathing suit and a pair of flip-flops for the beach. More clothes, a couple of books, some CDs. And the phone he had left there. The small display, the push buttons. An object from the past. An intersection of time that creates an opening. And now even the conviction that selling the house can serve to close that chapter forever begins to falter under the weight of that small object and everything it holds, saved in its internal memory.

Something about it knocks the breath out of him, just thinking about it.

There are messages from Alice. Her texts. Since that night, he has never come so close to her. And now he feels that he can't avoid it. Because his return, all of it, seems to converge at this point.

He has to get through here, to leave it behind forever.

The phone is still attached to the charger cable. He plugs the adapter into the outlet and looks out the window while he waits for the display to light up. From here you can't see the street. That night, however, the blue flashing lights appeared through the trees.

He'd been lying on the couch. He hadn't felt like going to sleep. Alice was supposed to be there with him. Or so he had thought, that night when they would have had the whole house to themselves.

"That's it? Tonight the house is free?" she'd said to him in the car. "We'll go to your house and make love because your parents aren't there? The beach house! You think things never change, Enrico, or you pretend they haven't. That's your problem."

Enrico had been trying to make sense of those words as he lay on the couch staring at the shadows of the trees on the ceiling, stock-still in the absence of any wind. The sound of a car along the road. Another car. Yet another. The bluish flashes. At first it was just a feeling. Alice had climbed out of the old Beetle and returned home on foot. Blue lights. Cars going by at a time of night when no one ever passes. Just a feeling. Enrico got up and went to the window. The cell phone rang. Maurizio.

"Are you both at your house?" The use of that plural, the feeling takes on a form.

"I'm by myself."

"Alice isn't with you?"

"No, she was walking home."

"Did you hear from her?"

"No."

"I think something's happened, Erri. There are patrol cars and an ambulance."

"I'll try to call her and let you know."

But Alice's phone was off.

Enrico left the house. The Beetle. The gate. He retraced the route, cell phone in hand, sending a text.

Call me back.

Continuing to call, sending texts.

Call me back, it's important.

Calling again, sending texts, calling.

At first, just a feeling. Then the feeling is transformed, takes on the weight of anguish. It becomes a short circuit of images, of words, of a hypnotic repetition of them . . . *You'll see, it must be a coincidence . . . Don't even think about it . . . It's just a suggestion.*

Suggestion.

There were people going into the woods. Enrico wanted to roll down the window and ask someone what was going on. But he couldn't bring himself to do it.

Suggestion.

The patrol cars and the ambulance were stopped along the road, next to the woods. Enrico got out of the car and approached them. Everything is okay.

It was the eyes.

The look of a couple of people whom Enrico knew.

The way they looked at him.

It was like falling headlong, into those eyes.

A sound rouses him. He returns to the present. The beach house is a place of ghosts. Something is fluttering over the bookcase. He goes over, tries to push it, and manages to shift it. A big moth flies away from the top shelf, toward the window. It alights on the glass. Now it's a large dark triangle, drawn by the tenuous light of dusk that comes from outside. It had happened once before, long ago. At that same spot. He, who had never gotten along well with insects, had taken a rolled-up newspaper and had gone over to whack it.

"You know what they say about moths?" Alice was there, next to him.

"You have a story for everything?"

"It's something that has to do with the cult of the dead." Alice restrained the hand that held the rolled-up newspaper and moved close to the insect. "They say that a moth brings with it the spirit of a departed person who at night comes back to see us. That's why they occasionally enter houses. According to ancient folk beliefs, it's a soul that can't find peace and is looking for someone to say a prayer for it."

"I should say a prayer?"

"It depends." Alice caught the creature in her hand, just barely closing her fingers over its wings. "Some people make the sign of the cross, others spin around three times clockwise. If you know a magic formula, you can recite that." She walked over to the open window from which the moth had entered. "Or you can simply help it find its way home," she said, opening her fingers and lightly blowing on the insect, who eventually flew off toward the trees.

Now, however, Alice is gone. There is only Enrico's bad rapport with insects. Especially the kind that fly. He tries to do the same thing, more or less. Pulling his sweater up to cover his neck, an instinctive gesture dictated by the fear that something might slip in there, he approaches slowly, slides the window up, and leaves it wide open.

"That's the way out, but don't expect me to carry you there."

As he backs away from the moth, he sees that his old cell phone on the table has lit up. It's the signal he's been waiting for. It's now charged and turned on. What he's about to do will not be painless, but it can't be avoided. He picks up the phone, opens the message app, and sets the time machine in motion. He scrolls through, looking for one in particular that he remembers.

In no time, half an hour has gone by.

The last message he received from her. August 8, ten years ago. It's as if those words obliterated time. He's gripped by emotion. Something is knotted up inside his stomach, looking for a way out but can't find it. It's as if she were there. As if that message had just arrived, and the sender's name—Alice—weren't just the contents of a digital memory.

Then there are the others. The ones Enrico has never read.

The way has been cleared: he keeps going.

Messages that came in the days that followed. Friends who were looking for him. Friends who were wondering why. Friends who offered their time, their support, their encouragement. Messages received during the time the phone was still on, plugged in.

And then it happens.

Scrolling through those messages, finding names and numbers, which can be associated with faces, voices, Enrico finds something that should not be there. An inconsistency.

An error.

There is a message. The date is two weeks after Alice's death. And that's why it's completely absurd that the sender's name should be hers. Alice's.

I looked for you at the funeral, but you weren't there.

Time ruptures. Breathing stops. Day and night turn inside out.

Enrico tries to find the error. It's like a game. The picture is perfect, but a detail is wrong. Or rather, two.

His finger moves, an involuntary spasm, and he discovers another message.

The sender's name is still the same.

Alice.

I thought you wanted to know, and instead you chose to forget.

The phone slips out of his hand. Falls on the table. The sound is dull, it's plastic. Enrico slumps down on the chair. He picks up the phone again. Reads it once more. Puts it down again. Gets up again.

He looks out the window. The old trees, their leaves dry.

His head is spinning.

A joke. A bad joke.

Who?

Who had sent those messages?

He's dizzy. He leans against the back of the sofa. What was there to know? What should he have known? He feels his stomach exploding, the vomit rising in his throat, acidic. The bathroom door slams against the radiator as Enrico hunches over the toilet bowl.

Everything's all right. There must be an explanation. Calm down.

He rinses his face at the sink. Dries it with the towel. He turns on the light above the mirror. The pale face of someone who has just seen a ghost stares back. Or maybe he's the ghost? He goes back to the living room. A gust of cold air hits him. The window is still open.

The moth is gone.

Eleven

Mom seems agitated, Grandma, that friend of theirs is coming to dinner tonight.

Do you remember him?

A little, more like what I've heard.

But what is he doing there?

Mom says he came to sell the house because he doesn't want to go back there.

For her, it must be quite emotional, they were very close, almost like brother and sister.

She told me about it. Do you want me to say hello to her for you?

Never mind, don't tell anyone that we talk.

I'm going now, so I can help Mom get things ready.

Later you'll tell me all about it, okay?

Okay. Ciao, Grandma.

Chiara presses the "Off" button and slips the iPhone in the pocket of her jeans. She removes the earbuds. She isn't allowed to wear them at the table anyway. And tonight, in any case, she wants to listen.

She heard the doorbell ring and knows that the guest has arrived. She pulls a sweater on over her T-shirt and heads for the stairs. She leans over a little to see below. She hears her parents' voices and a voice she doesn't recognize. They say hello, the normal things that people say on such occasions: *Time doesn't seem to have passed for you and yet damn! How many years has it been?* and *Let's make sure it's not that long next time.* But it's clear that if that guy came all the way here to get rid of the house, he has no intention of coming back.

Chiara takes a few steps down the stairs—and sits down. She likes to observe people without being seen. Her father and Enrico are in the living room, her mother went to the kitchen to get the prosecco from the fridge and the tray with the vegetable canapés she prepared.

"These are the *babies*?" Enrico says, picking up a photograph from a shelf. It's a picture taken in London last year, when they went to see Margherita. Chiara and her sister are hugging and smiling in a park. Chiara likes that photo. She used it for her sister's profile picture on her iPhone. Her sister is beautiful, everyone says so. Long hair, full lips. She's tall, taller than Chiara, who year after year sees the illusion of becoming like her fade even more.

"Yeah, the *babies*," Maurizio says.

"They're beautiful."

"We don't see Margherita much, but we know that things are going well for her, so it's okay with us."

"Why London?"

"Well, at the time we had the chance to send her. It was a great opportunity and she . . . How should I put it . . . Wasn't very happy here."

"Too small a town."

"Yeah, something like that."

Her father is speaking in that slurred way that happens when he drinks. He must be on his fourth gin and tonic at least.

"And Chiara?" the guest asks.

"Chiara wants to go be with her sister."

They smile.

Betti returns, carrying the tray with the appetizers and glasses of prosecco. She sets the tray on the table and hands the glasses to the men in her life. The tinkling of crystal. Her mother glances toward the stairs and Chiara knows that she's about to call her. So she goes down.

"Chiara, do you remember Enrico?" her mother asks her.

"How can she remember me?" Enrico says.

"A little. Not much, though."

There's a moment's pause. An air bubble.

"Shall we sit down?" Betti says, breaking the silence.

It's strange how adults always manage to talk about something else. To avoid names and facts as though they were obstacles along a course. No one reminisces about the past, for fear they might end up talking about that girl, Alice.

Chiara watches her mother closely. She starts to relax after the second prosecco, after she's covered the entire table with plates and saucers and little bowls and sauces and condiments. Little by little they loosen up, as if they were slowly beginning to recognize one another. A memory or two enters their conversation: "That summer . . . That time . . . That night when . . ." Until at some point the inevitable arrives: "Alice was there that night too." And it's Enrico who says it. Then they go on talking, telling stories. Chiara remembers when she was little and their house was always filled with people: all the friends who stayed for dinner, chatting, listening to music. She looks at her mother, whose eyes, as usual, are teary. It's to be expected. It's strange how all this seems to make them happy. Because when adults talk about the past, it's sad, Chiara thinks. They talk about things they no longer have, about people they haven't seen, about friends lost along the way. How can they not be crushed by sadness? How can they not be afraid of all that lost time?

Chiara stays with them for a while, until she can tell from their conversation that they aren't going to say anything more that night. Only then does she say good night and go upstairs. She lies down on the bed, turns on her computer to select a movie, and picks up the phone to tell her grandmother about the evening. No one knows that she's in touch with her. If her mother found out, she would make a scene.

When she hears Enrico leaving, she goes to the window, not letting them see her from below. They're in the garden. Their last exchange with one another. Her mother laughs and continues wiping her eyes. She's hopeless. Enrico came on foot because he'd felt like walking, but now her father wants to drive him back.

If the police stop him and make him take the balloon test, they'll take away his license.

As the car pulls away, Betti remains standing there. She draws her cardigan around her. Then she looks up at the sky. Chiara knows that her mother likes stars. She sees her half close her eyes and smile. She follows her as she goes back into the house and knows that for at least an hour now there will be a clatter of dishes and glasses and running water and silverware tossed about between the sink and the dishwasher basket. Things which, for that matter, will already have been washed by hand before the dishwasher is even turned on; it's one of those things about her mother that she will never understand.

◆ ◆ ◆

"Here we are," Maurizio says. He took the long way to show him something. They get out of the car. In front of them, a hill with a fenced-in area. "The construction will take place here. Cubic volumes transferred from the urban center and applied here to build the houses and facilities and golf course between the hill and the valley on the other side. A significant investment, but safe, see? All you have to do is put in the money and you'll double your investment, but it's no use. It took me years to form these friendships, to get into this circle, but she doesn't give a shit."

"How come she doesn't talk to her mother anymore?"

Maurizio rummages through his jacket pockets for the pack of cigarettes. When he finds it, he pulls it out and takes one, twirls it around a bit between his fingers.

"They had an argument, a bad one. Her mother is a pain in the ass, but all she'd have to do is put up a couple of apartments as security for the loan and I could get into the association." He puts the cigarette between his lips and lights it, then blows out a thick cloud of smoke. "But it won't happen. And you know Betti, when she makes up her mind about something, there's nothing you can do. She won't listen to reason, even if it means fucking up the project of a lifetime." He again offers the pack to Enrico, who refuses. "You quit? Good for you, this stuff will kill you. But, as they say, something or other will . . . You know, we're not really that sweet little family picture we served you at dinner."

"No one is."

"Yeah." Maurizio takes a deep drag. "And I'm left here watching this fucking hill and all that money that could be mine, all that work I did for years getting into that circle of loaded assholes. Fuck it. Life is full of missed opportunities."

"What are you talking about?"

Maurizio inhales, making the tip flare up, and blows the smoke out in puffs, trying to make big rings.

"Nothing, stuff from long ago."

"I got two messages from Alice's number." Enrico says it just like that. The words slip out by themselves, casually.

"What? When?"

"A few weeks after that night."

"Why are you telling me this now?"

"Because I just found them."

"Meaning?"

"The box you brought me also contained the cell phone. It automatically saved the messages in the phone's memory. A number of messages came in over the days following that night. A bunch of people telling me things. And there were those two messages, sent from Alice's phone."

"I remember that thing about her phone."

"What?"

"They searched for it, but didn't find it. You didn't know that?"

"They didn't find her phone?"

"You didn't follow the news much when you left, did you, Erri?"

"No."

"They didn't find it. But in any event the case was closed quickly. There wasn't a whole lot to investigate."

"But those messages were sent later."

"Are you worried about it?"

"It gave me a strange feeling, as you can imagine."

"I'll send my security guard over. He'll check out the house, take a look, and we'll see. I have some idea as to who might be busting your chops, including the visit you had today in the garden, before I got there."

"Sandro?"

"Bingo."

"You think he had the phone?"

"I don't know, but I'm sure it was him this morning at your house."

"Why?"

"Because on my way there I passed his car."

"Why didn't you tell me?"

"Because you already seemed stressed out, and I didn't want to add more tension. Sandro hasn't turned out well, but I don't think he can cause you any trouble. Still, I'll call my security guard."

"What do you mean he 'hasn't turned out well'?"

"After Giancarlo died in prison, he was left alone. His mother never recovered from that hideous night. She stayed shut up in the house and they say her mind is no longer all there. And Sandro let himself go more or less. Said to hell with it all, started doing drugs and dealing. Nowadays he's one of the many specters heroin has left to drift around in this shitty place."

The hill. The night. Silence.

"Do you mind taking me home?" Enrico asks. "I'm a little tired."

"No problem."

Filthy undershirt stained with blood. Biceps shiny with sweat. Unkempt beard and thinning hair. Icy stare. Detective Lieutenant John McClane in *Die Hard* has Bruce Willis's sharp-edged face. The sound comes through an earbud stuck in the ear of Enzo Porretta, the security guard employed by the local real-estate agency. His favorite movie is that first one. The images play out on the screen of the small DVD player propped up on the dashboard of the company car. A giant bag of corn chips rests between his legs. A long straw extends from a can of Fanta Lemon, secured in its proper place on the armrest; Enzo made it by joining four straws together, so he could drink without removing the can from its holder. He's wearing a short-sleeved shirt with the logo of the security service for which he works, a size too small, to show off his biceps, but when he's seated he has to undo the buttons over his belly. He shares Lieutenant McClane's thinning hair, but his face is less angular, tending more to fat, with a hint of an unkempt beard, or rather stubble that has never grown well. At night he goes out on his rounds, for which the agency's clients pay a lot more money than he ever sees, and leaves the calling cards that confirm he's been by. Sometimes he stops and watches part of a movie, like now. Behind him lay a disastrous past as a municipal police officer and a contract that was not renewed due to a series of gunshots that exploded in front of a supermarket, when he thought he saw a thief fleeing. But it doesn't matter: the agency's badge is way cooler, resembling that of an American policeman. Besides, he can always say he is a former police officer who is now a private investigator. Now that McClane has an automatic weapon, and announces the fact to his enemies with "NOW I HAVE A MACHINE GUN HO-HO-HO" stamped on the T-shirt that is his touch of class, Enzo knows the best part of the film is about to start. But just then his cell phone lights up in its holder on the dashboard. Enzo is forced to let go of the handful of corn chips that he had just scooped out of the bag. He rinses his mouth with a little Fanta Lemon, grabs the Bluetooth earbud hanging by the phone, puts it in the other ear—so that he now has the phone in one ear and *Die Hard* in the other—and presses the green button.

"Porretta," he says, responding with his last name like they do in the movies, even though his surname is sadly unsuited to that kind of thing.

"Enzo, the guy from Beta Realty called for some extra drive-bys to check on a house."

"Roger."

"What?"

"Roger."

"What the hell is that?"

"Okay, okay, which house?"

The guy from the agency tells him the address on Via delle Ortiche.

"Roger."

"Again?"

"It means 'I got it.'"

"So then tell me you got it."

"I got it."

"And don't do anything stupid. Beta is a good client, you know. Okay?"

"Ro . . . Got it."

He ends the call. He hangs the earbud back in its place. He shuts off the DVD player and puts it on the passenger seat. He stuffs a handful of chips in his mouth, closes the bag, and slides it into the compartment inside the armrest. He wipes corn chip crumbs off his hands, and takes a moist towelette from a compartment under the steering wheel. A sip of Fanta Lemon. He tightens his lips the way Bruce Willis does, looks around, thinks about how everything would be different if there were lighted skyscrapers surrounding him instead of these sad, discolored apartment buildings with clothes hanging outside and pots of basil on the balconies. He narrows his eyes. He imagines his tough-guy look and avoids the rearview mirror so as not to break the spell. He turns on the ignition, puts the car in gear, and goes to do his dirty work.

Betti's mind is blank. The evening has left her sleepless. But it's not just that.

After straightening up the living room and kitchen, she opened the cabinet door where she keeps the tins of herbal teas and chose the fennel-seed tea that reduces gastrointestinal distress. She filled the tea infuser, heated the water in the electric kettle, and poured it into the cup. With a gentle, circular motion, she stirred the tea ball, watching it release its wake of color and transform the hot water into the drink that will help her relax. It is in such gestures, repeated each and every time in the same way, that she finds her way to a state of nonthinking, of silence and ataraxia, the relief of a serenity induced by a ritual of small, intimate acts, comforting in the fact that they are already preset in an unvarying and recurring pattern that preserves their identicalness.

The aroma of the fennel rises lightly, wafted by the steam.

Betti checks the time. Maurizio and Enrico left quite some time ago. Maybe there's a little jealousy in thinking that they owe their friendship to her, because she was Enrico's friend first, and it was she who later met Maurizio, and it is through her that the two men met. But that typical male complicity naturally and callously excludes all women from the after-dinner ritual of brandy and cigars. Even if it's only having one last beer while leaning against the hood of the car or taking a piss in the open countryside. But it's not just that.

There's a worm of doubt working its way in, gnawing at her, boring into the silence, in that absence of thought resonant with the echo of an evening that is almost surreal in its relationship with time.

She can't help it. She picks up the phone, retrieves a message that Enrico sent that afternoon to say hello and tell her that they would see each other in a few hours, and hits "Reply."

Excuse me, I hope I didn't wake you. Is Maurizio still with you?

Enrico had sat out in the garden for a while, accompanied by half a bottle of Lagavulin he'd found in the house, in the bar cart. He's always enjoyed certain moments of solitude. When he went back inside, he closed the door gently, hearing the lock click. He took off his shoes, sat on the sofa, stretched his arms along the back, and propped his feet on the coffee table in front of him. He threw his head back and his gaze fell on the ceiling. He stayed in that position, just staring at the ceiling for a while. Then he lowered his eyes and she was there, in front of him, perched on the coffee table.

"It doesn't seem like so much time has passed," he says.

"How does it make you feel?" Alice asks him.

"Coming back here?"

"Yeah."

"It's strange."

"How so?"

"Like finding a piece of myself, which now I'm no longer so sure I want to discard."

"You mean the house?"

"Maybe."

"Your friends?"

"They've changed."

"You've all changed. Maybe you're the one who has changed the most."

"Do you still want to go to Biarritz, to see the ocean?"

The sound of the cell phone. A text message. Enrico's thoughts scatter in an instant. The coffee table is empty, there's nobody there anymore. He gets up, searches for the phone in his jacket pocket. It's Betti's number.

She asks if Maurizio is still with him.

No, we left each other a while ago. Is everything all right?

He sets the phone down on the table while waiting for her to text back and pours another glass of scotch. The sound announcing her reply comes quickly.

Sorry, everything's fine. I just heard his car.

But it's not true. Betti turns the phone off. She tries to fill the void, which on certain nights yawns beneath her feet, by inhaling the scent of fennel. She switches off the kitchen light and carries the cup to bed. Under the covers, it all seems less painful at times. Maurizio's side of the bed is empty. He'll come back later and try to take a shower without waking her, to rinse off that smell that doesn't belong in this house.

The tea is still quite hot. Betti already feels the illusion of relief in her stomach.

The black car is moving very slowly. Its headlights are off. It's right in front of his gate, from here you can't see anything else. It pulls up. He's in the house. He's back. Better to turn off the engine. Remain in the dark, watching. Enrico left his car outside the gate. He has a station wagon now that must have cost at least forty thousand euro. *I wonder if he got rid of that old trendy clunker, the convertible Beetle, as soon as he returned to Rome, while here, they were burying Alice—because of him.*

The sound of a car. Someone coming. No problem, he just has to duck down in the seat to avoid being seen.

It must just be passing by.

Negative, Lieutenant McClane. There's nobody here. All quiet. Cars parked along the street. No suspicious movement.

Security guard Enzo Porretta steps out of the car and clips the key to his belt, next to the flashlight. He hikes up his pants to cover the generous swathe of exposed pale ass and looks around, narrowing his eyes to ruthless slits. From his shirt pocket, he pulls out an agency card. He crosses the street accompanied by the clomp of his boots and the rustling of a nonexistent wind, the echo of some Western movie whose name he doesn't remember. He approaches the gate slowly. He slips the card in a crack beside the lock and turns around.

All quiet. Doesn't it seem *too* quiet? *Central, we're gonna take a closer look, these shitty terrorist bastards hole up like sewer rats.*

He takes the flashlight from his belt, clicks on the switch with an abrupt motion, and aims the beam of light on the ground, as if he had drawn a *katana*, while his eyes look elsewhere.

They asked for an extra drive-by, Central. And we'll give it to 'em.

He points the flashlight into the station wagon parked next to the gate. He scrutinizes the interior, looking for something. Anything that seems out of place. Nothing. All run-of-the-mill. He bends down to look underneath.

And it's at that moment that he hears the screeching tires of another car taking off like a shot.

He leaps up. With all the feline swiftness that his abundant avoirdupois will allow, he races around the parked car and aims his flashlight onto the street. A black car is speeding away. The bastard got the better of him. Or at least he thought he did.

Everything under control, Central. No problem.

"Now I have your license-plate number, you piece of shit. HO-HO-HO."

PART TWO

WALKING THROUGH THE WOODS

One

Imagine a house, with two floors, surrounded by other similar houses, each with a small garden and a path leading to a garage. In the garden is a gazebo with a small table and a few scattered chairs. Some colored lights, a little music, somewhat dated so that when listening to it you can say, "Remember that?" The urge to have fun now faded, the kind of fun that no longer comes as naturally as it did before, because it requires an extra effort. Now that evenings when you can enjoy yourself are planned, and you can't afford the luxury of not enjoying them. Picture Betti. Try to follow her movements tonight. Watch her as she moves among the others, with a bottle of beer in her hand. She left the babies with her mother and ordered herself to have fun. She seems happy as she talks with her friends, welcomes them in the garden, and shows them where they can help themselves to appetizers, cold pasta, frozen pizza, and drinks. Colored paper plates, colored paper cups, colored paper napkins. Try to take a step back, enlarge the picture. See the other people standing at the edges of the image? Does it really look like they're having fun? And doesn't Betti's enthusiasm start to seem out of place, now that they're all nothing more than little fish swimming in too small a pond?

Now a yellow Beetle arrives. Let's move closer again, just enough to see me and Enrico get out of the car and walk up to the gate of

Maurizio and Betti's house. I'm wearing a pale-blue blouse. It's the one that Sandro will later recognize, when he sees it in the woods, soiled with mud.

Enrico honks the horn and raises a hand to wave. When Maurizio looks in our direction, I look the other way to avoid meeting his eyes. We go inside with them, stand among them. Get something to drink and sit on the glider in the garden, next to Paolino, the pale, gangly guy in a short-sleeved shirt with a cell phone in its case hanging from his belt. As soon as he notices you, he'll say, "What a night, huh?" because he always says that. But, then, since he usually doesn't say anything else, he'll leave you in peace to take it all in.

Enrico must have noticed that Betti is a little revved up. He goes over to her and they start moving to a song by R.E.M., "Losing My Religion." Now that you're up close you can read in their eyes that complicity that I sometimes envied. Still, it's not enough. It wasn't enough. Not even for them. That veil, however subtle, remained. He wasn't aware of it, she decided it was so.

She knows.

And where am I? I'd gone into the house, looking for the bathroom. So I said.

Instead I find Maurizio, in the kitchen, who, with the excuse of going to get cold beers from the fridge, was waiting for me. What follows is a dialogue from a badly written film script. You can copy and paste it right here. He says he wants to stop playing these games, no more subterfuges, that he loves me and wants to tell her so, that what happened between us is not anyone's fault but it happened and so on, that he's no longer happy with his life, that for too long he's stood by responsibilities that basically he didn't even want to assume, that he wants to live again, that in me he sees his life as it could be and that he's sick and tired of just watching it from a distance. And then I say that it's all wrong, because I made a mistake, I screwed up without meaning to, that I've decided to tell Enrico about it, but that I'm a shit because all day I didn't have the guts to do it.

I move away, he grabs me by the arm, I turn and . . .

"We need beers."

Betti is at the kitchen door. She smiles. Maybe she heard.

Sitting on the glider, next to Paolino, you saw Betti dancing just before, then at one point stop. She looked in the house. You saw her smile at Enrico and tell him something about the beers. But, since you are not involved in the party and are aware of your role as observer, you were able to see what even Enrico hadn't seen. The smile that wilted on Betti's lips.

You went into the house with her. You saw there was someone in the kitchen. You heard voices speaking, as yet indistinct. You approached. You recognized some scraps of that poorly written dialogue and saw when he tried to stop me . . .

"We need beers."

Not knowing how to get out of it, I open the fridge, take a few beers, and carry them outside. My head is spinning. I have to talk to Enrico. I have to be the one to tell him.

He's in the garden. He smiles at me.

I feel dirty. I desperately want to clean myself. I go back inside and go upstairs to the bathroom. I strip off my clothes.

"You okay?" Maurizio again, outside the door.

"Please go away."

I start crying. I feel the cold water on my face. I'm shivering. I don't know what I'm doing. I put my clothes on over my wet body. I open the door, and Maurizio is there with his fucking beer in hand, looking at me like I am crazy.

"What the hell are you doing?" he asks me.

I push past him back down the stairs.

I go outside and tell Enrico I want to leave. That I need to talk to him about something. And that's how it all happens.

Two

Enrico just didn't understand why that perfect world of his had stopped working. It was so clear that I would move to Rome with him. It was so clear that this would be the outcome, the next step. Completely linear, with no change of direction or sudden swerves. Enrico's perfect world was a happy, colorful toy train—its route marked by two solid tracks—from which to enjoy the scenery, admire the shapes of the trees, fill your eyes with the beauty all around you. So it was impossible for him to understand why someone would decide to get off. And maybe I made a mistake. I should have told him about Maurizio right away, rather than starting at the end, with the decision to be on my own for a while. Because Enrico's reaction was such that all other arguments were unlikely.

We were on the way back from the party. Enrico was driving me home. He'd wanted me to spend the night with him, but I didn't feel like it, not after I told him what I had to tell him. I was talking, trying to put together the speech I had practiced to myself thousands of times, but that suddenly seemed so confused. At one point, he pulled the car over, turned to me without taking his hands off the wheel, and asked, "Is there someone else?"

Was there? Had there been? Was that the reason? I couldn't respond, and my hesitation triggered something in Enrico that I hadn't seen in all the years I'd known him. Shortness of breath, eyes brimming with tears that he struggled to hold back. I'd really hurt him and I was sorry, truly. But he came down hard on me and, in the end, I don't think I deserved it, not that way at least. I couldn't say anything. He didn't give me a chance. Finally, I opened the car door and stepped out into the road. I had no idea why I'd done it. Maybe to get some air, escape the sound of his voice, spewing out words he had no right to say to me. I walked away. Maybe that's when I decided to return home on my own. I don't know. The idea was barely formed. I saw the woods and I realized that if I cut straight through, I would reach the provincial road to Carrubo and from there I would go straight home. It wasn't far.

Enrico did nothing. Maybe deep inside I hoped that he'd get out, that he would call after me. That he would even try and stop me, grab my arms, hold me back, before he finally heard me, accepted things.

But he did not. He stayed in the car. I saw him with his head lowered, defeated, crushed by too strong a blow. It was my fault that he stayed there. But seeing him that way, all his defenses down, I thought it would be best to leave him by himself. And that was why, in the end, I made the decision I did.

I turned to the woods and slipped into the trees.

When I heard Enrico's car start and found myself alone, I began to calm down. I decided not to think about any of it until the next day. I decided to put the things that were said and not said out of my head. The woods weren't dense in that area. I liked to go there, especially in summer. I was reminded of an old song by The Cure, "One More Time," that I always listened to as I came home from school; I would get off a stop ahead to do the last stretch on foot and pass through these woods. I loved The Cure. I loved that song and that album, and I think the desire to hear it again was one of the last happy thoughts of my life. Because at that moment, as I thought about the strange red album cover and the instrumental intro to the first song, I heard a noise. Someone was there, close to me. And turning around I saw him.

That pasty face of his, twisted into a sick expression, appeared before me like a ghost.

The Half-Wit.

He lived in that little cabin in the woods, not far from here. I hadn't thought about it, that's all. It may sound absurd, but the fact that that area, so familiar to me, could become a place of danger, because of the Half-Wit, was a thought that hadn't even crossed my mind.

But now here he was. Staring at me with that blank, wide-eyed look.

He was leaning against a tree. He still had that cap of his on his head. I turned and started walking quickly away. Then I heard him coming behind me. I started running. In an instant fear devoured everything else. The woods seemed suddenly vast and menacing, as if they wanted to close up around me, imprison me there, alone with that maniac. I reached into my pocket and pulled out my cell phone.

I frantically scrolled through the last numbers I'd called to find Enrico's number, thinking maybe he was still close, but I realized that I had picked up the wrong phone earlier that evening. I had grabbed the phone that was used to take reservations at the restaurant. It was identical to mine. It wasn't the first time I'd gotten them mixed up. So Enrico's number wasn't there, and I never memorized numbers. But Sandro's number was saved on that phone.

I kept running, even though I had the feeling that the Half-Wit was no longer behind me. I slowed down for a moment, just long enough to open the contacts list and select my brother's number.

The phone rang and rang, but he didn't answer.

I sent him a text.

Call me. A

I added the *A* because the number wasn't mine, and seeing the restaurant's number, Sandro would at the very least call home. If there was the chance of doing something stupid, my brother did not usually pass it up.

I tried him again, but it was no use.

I went on running. Maybe the Half-Wit wasn't so fast, I reasoned, trying to calm down some. But I couldn't stop seeing that ghost-white face of his.

When Sandro didn't answer a third time, I left him a message.

"Where the hell are you, Sandro? I'm walking back and that fucking maniac is following me. Call me back, otherwise I'll have to call home, and if *he* comes he'll kill him and I don't want to talk to him about this. Come on, Sandro, call me. I'm almost to the road near the bend."

I don't know how long I ran, but I kept going, never looking back. Time seemed interminable. When I realized that I was close to the road, I turned around, but the Half-Wit was nowhere to be seen. I could have called Sandro back and told him to forget it, but I was still scared and I wouldn't have minded seeing my brother's car arrive. I approached the road, catching my breath.

When the car's headlights sprang from around the curve, I leaned into the road to be seen. The headlights slowed. The car stopped.

But it wasn't Sandro's.

It all happened so quickly.

It's strange, but the last thing I remember is a thought. An apartment that has never existed. I am there, with a cup of tea, an old couch with a book propped on it, my stereo with CDs stacked on the floor, a window steamy with condensation. I can't figure out where this place is because I can't see anything through the window. Everything looks white. I should get closer, maybe wipe the glass or open the window and look out. I'm by myself. From the stereo, I hear Eddie Vedder's voice singing "Black." I'm wearing my heavy socks, and there's a warm blanket on that sofa, which is just waiting for me to curl up on it to finish that book. It's a strange feeling, maybe I don't fully understand it, but I have the impression that I have never felt so happy. That there is nothing else I need. So I decide to forget about the window. It's cold outside. I don't feel like opening it, and in the end knowing what's out there isn't so important. What's important is what's in here. I clasp the cup in my hands as the tea's aroma fills the room. I walk over to the couch. I lie down and cover my legs with the blanket. It's so nice and warm. So soft. I pick up the book and start to read.

And without even realizing it, I fall asleep.

Three

Enrico has that half bottle of Lagavulin floating around in his head. Lost somewhere in the night, he gets up from the couch, opens the fridge, takes big gulps from the bottle of mineral water, and looks at the clock, a reflex that has nothing to do with wanting to know what time it is. There is only one thought around which his mind revolves.

The messages.

"I thought you wanted to know, and instead you chose to forget."

Was it Sandro who'd left them? Was it like Maurizio said? Was that the explanation? Why would he do it? Why use Alice's phone? If Sandro had indeed sent those messages, why would he keep Alice's phone? To torment him? And know what? What was it he should have wanted to know?

An obsessive thought. Like a wave, always the same, which produces an identical roar each time it swells and breaks on the shore. Then he checks the clock again without noticing what time it is, opens the fridge again, reaches for the same bottle, goes back to the couch where he left his jacket, and checks to see if there are any messages, from Giulia or anyone else who now seems far away. He takes the same steps around the room, circling the only thing that can pull him out of the obsession that he is only now becoming aware of. The old phone is in the center of the coffee table. A faint nocturnal light comes through the window, gently caressing it. Clunky, so rapidly outdated in the way that is typical of objects of this type. Enrico sits down at the table. He leans his elbows on it, intertwines his hands, and rests his chin on them. He knows what he is about to do. Putting it off any longer has the uncertainty of hesitation, but it is merely preparatory, a deep breath before taking action. The SIM is disabled by now. He's about to get up and get his phone out of his jacket pocket when he's surprised to find it already there, in his hand. He enters Alice's number and presses the call button. It starts ringing. In the air a signal travels in search of a reply, but it comes up against a closed door, and a recorded voice says something about a number that does not exist or words that he would have understood better had he not been in the company of half a bottle of Scotch. So then he writes a text message:

Are you still there? I haven't forgotten anything. What should I know? (Enrico)

He hits "Send," then gets up, checks his watch that could have been stopped for days without him being aware of it, goes back to the kitchen, opens the fridge again, and as he drinks from the bottle of mineral water, wonders what sense it makes to send a message ten years back in time. What sense does any of this make, and why did he even stay here instead of just returning on Monday to conclude his business with the agency.

He sets his phone down on the coffee table, next to the other one. It's the dead of night, unlikely that anyone will answer. What time is it? He doesn't know. But it's late. Maybe he'll be able to sleep a few hours before morning comes. He always sleeps very little, no more than four hours, then he spends the rest of the night on the couch. Sometimes he reads, sometimes he looks for something on television, always with the sound turned off to avoid waking Giulia. When he's really tired, he resorts to some magic little pill that helps him conquer his insomnia, but when he wakes up he feels weird, unnatural. Too easy to know when it was that nights started being so long and unbearable. If in ten years he hasn't yet been able to sleep, is it any wonder why he hasn't returned home and decided to stay here?

He goes back to the kitchen, opens the fridge, takes the bottle, and drinks from it in big gulps. He crumples the empty bottle so it will take up less space in the recycling bin. He opens the fridge again and grabs another bottle. He opens it, drinks from it, and puts it back on the shelf. He checks the clock. He rolls down all the shutters, creating total darkness, the sole condition in which he ever manages to fall asleep. He lies down on the couch.

He feels his body sinking into the cushions and feels the warmth of the hours of sleep approaching.

He closes his eyes and lets himself relax.

He doesn't yet know that his return to town has already had consequences. That things that had remained buried for so many years are about to come to light.

Four

Fabiana's body was a perfect black silhouette in the white luminosity of the strobe light that flashed behind her. A profile that Sandro could mentally fill in with everything he needed, being familiar with every single detail, every inch of that form.

Before arriving at the Tortuga, the discotheque where Fabiana worked as a cube dancer, he had spent an hour lifting weights in his room, to make his veins stand out and his biceps and pecs appear to bulge from his tight black T-shirt. Touch up the peroxided soul patch, add the diamond earring. If Alice had seen him, she would have said something about the utter "crassness" of certain choices, or as she calls them, "aesthetic solutions." But, fortunately, the city boy from Rome had taken her to a party.

Once he entered the club, Sandro headed straight to the bar to get his first mojito, something to hold in his hand so he could flex his arms, showing off his biceps.

That night he had a precise objective: to leave with Fabiana.

He had met her at the gym. And checked her out. She was little more than twenty and had already had a few auditions to dance on television. While under the weights, Sandro eavesdropped on her and on some of the other girls to gather a little information about her. Once he would have asked his sister for help, but now she went around putting on airs, acting like an intellectual. And Fabiana was the type of girl whom Alice would call vacuous or stupid, because ever since she got that useless degree, she thought she was better than everybody else. According to her, everyone was shallow and wasting their time on insignificant things. Alice had become a pain in the ass. Worse than the hysterical, frustrated teachers whom Sandro was glad to be rid of when he finished high school.

Fabiana, however, was like him. She spent her evenings on the workout equipment to shape her body, because your body is your temple and you need to take care of it and worship it. And when she went to the pulleys, where she worked on her thighs and glutes, Sandro always made sure to be at the rowing machine, right in front of the mirror in which he could admire her in all her splendor, as her muscles contracted under the tension. But it was the expression that the effort and exertion sketched on her face that drove Sandro crazy, since he imagined that same expression as the result of a different kind of exertion. And the rowing machine was the ideal place to surrender to those fantasies, in part because while he was sitting down, he could conceal the erection that Fabiana regularly aroused in him.

Then one evening she'd happened to get a cramp in her calf, and he had rushed over to grab her foot to help her stretch it out. In an instant, he'd managed to erase all distance between them. And the feeling that she hadn't really had a cramp and that she had made it up just to break the ice was even more exciting. Anyway, that's how they'd met. The rest followed accordingly. She told him about her auditions, that she had once met TV host Paolo Bonolis and that they sometimes texted one another, that hairdressers at the television studios have an edge because they are always up-to-date on current trends, that once she was almost picked, but then they passed over her for another girl favored by the host, Maria De Filippi. That all in all it was hard, but that to stand out in life you have to believe in yourself, otherwise you'd end up like so many others and not do fuck-all. And at the Tortuga, with his mojito in hand, Sandro had the terrible feeling that he was one of those others. Because Fabiana was up there sliding up and down a pole like Catwoman, while he sipped that crap full of crushed leaves that he would have gladly traded for a can of San Pellegrino Chinotto.

The plan was to hang around and wait for Fabiana to take a break, then approach her and ask her if maybe she'd like to have breakfast somewhere afterward. Then they would stop and get a couple of croissants and he'd take her to the beach to wait for sunrise. He would slip a little soft music into the car's stereo, a system with a kick-ass subwoofer, and say one of those things that usually make girls melt, of which he had a substantial and reliable collection.

But the first obstacle appeared a few minutes later. His name was Roman. He worked for Sandro's father. He was Giancarlo's foreman, the Albanian who scraped together workers for the construction site. Sandro saw him and some of the other guys come in, all together. As soon as Roman spotted him, he slapped him on the shoulder and dragged him over to the others, who gathered close like a herd that had just found its leader. They danced around edgily and clapped their hands like a tribal ritual. Sandro knew that he should buy them all a drink, because that's what his father would have done, and if he wanted them to respect him as much as they did Giancarlo, and not just because he was his son, he had to behave the same way.

Amid the deafening music, Sandro drained his mojito, handed the glass to a guy in the group whose name he didn't remember but who must have been Polish or something like that, and called them all over to the bar. When they realized that he was buying them drinks, they lifted him off the ground and carried him around triumphantly. There were at least a dozen of them. While the waiter was mixing the cocktails, Sandro saw a guy jump onto the cube with Fabiana. He knew him by sight—they called him Cedro, which was maybe his last name, he wasn't sure.

"If you want, I'll go over there and break his knee." Roman's voice in his ear carried the reek of one of those crappy garlic things that he must have eaten beforehand with the others.

"Never mind, it's only pussy." What was he supposed to say? That he needed their help to get her? Because Giancarlo is a man who knows how to make people respect him, but his asshole son needs someone to help him round up a cunt so he can fuck her? "There's better than that around."

"How about we go find a little beaver at Gilda's?" one of them said.

"What the hell? Are you all horny tonight?"

"They all have a fucking hard-on, Sandro," Roman said. "If I don't let them get their rocks off, they don't do good work."

According to Roman that was supposed to be a joke. Sandro gave a faint laugh and guessed at what would follow. That if he took them to Gilda's, with five hundred euros, he would earn what his father wanted him to earn from the workers. And maybe Giancarlo would even pay him back, happy that he had taken the initiative.

And so Fabiana remained a missed opportunity. He glanced back one last time before he left. He had the feeling that Cedro would be the one to end up on the beach with her tonight, along with the warm croissants and soft music, and that she would find a way to thank him for the lovely evening.

"You're the greatest, Sandro. You're my idol." Again, the Polish guy, or whatever he was, who must have guessed where they would be spending the rest of the night and was already wide eyed, a hand in his pocket stroking his dick.

Five

The little cabin in the woods where the Half-Wit lived looked like it belonged in some children's fairy tale. The one where the ogre lives, that you should stay away from. Stone walls and a sloping, red-tiled roof. A small pergola in front of the door, along with a broken-down rocking chair, which sometimes moved by itself as if there were someone in it. An open window with a screen torn in a few places. A shovel, always propped against the door.

A yellowish lamp, with moths dancing around it when turned on.

The Half-Wit had just returned. He was still breathing hard after running through the woods. He was scared. Sitting on the bed, goggle eyed, he swung his head from side to side. Bent over like that, he seemed even bigger. His huge hands gripped his knees. His mouth was set in a tense grimace.

When things were too complicated, he got stuck. Sometimes they found him that way, stock-still, head swaying, because he didn't know which bucket to put the mortar in.

But he didn't mean to scare her. He just wanted to tell her that he wouldn't scare her anymore and that he wouldn't do that thing that even Mama said he shouldn't do. She said Jesus saw him, but he did it anyway, because when it itched, he just couldn't resist and he was a bad boy.

But the girl got scared. That big, rotten, ugly head of mine, just like Mama said before she raised her hands, she was always raising her hands, because I always made a mess, like when I was playing cards and knocked over the glasses because otherwise I drew my card too slowly and then it wasn't worth playing Briscola that way. But the girl got scared and instead Sandro—who played with the ball when he was a little boy and I said to him, "Sandro, will you throw me the ball?"—Sandro, the son of Giancarlone, who cares about me and gives me a house and feeds me and gives me work, which otherwise, with that big, rotten, ugly head of mine, like Mama said before she raised her hands, she was always raising her hands because I always made a mess, like when I was playing cards and knocked over the glasses because otherwise I drew my card too slowly and then it wasn't worth playing Briscola that way. But the girl got scared because I scared her and instead I shouldn't have done that because Sandro—who played with the ball when he was a little boy and I said to him, "Sandro, will you throw me the ball?"—Sandro, the son of Giancarlone, told me not to do that and I did it anyway, big, rotten, ugly head of mine, like Mama said before she raised her hands, she was always raising her hands because I always made a mess, and if the girl got scared now, the son of Giancarlone who cares about me, no, I mean Sandro who played with the ball when he was a little boy, Giancarlone's son will cut off my weenie, he'll do that thing with the shears because he told me to leave her alone and I left her alone and I wanted to tell her that I would leave her alone, that I saw her alone in the woods at night, and I wanted to tell her that from now on I would leave her alone. The girl got scared but I wanted to tell her. The girl started running but why are you running when there's no way I can keep up with you. I tried to run after her, Jesus knows I tried to run because Jesus, Mama said before she raised her hands, she was always raising her hands because I always made a mess, like when I was playing cards, Jesus knows I just wanted to tell her that I wouldn't bother her anymore, that if I felt like doing that thing that Mama always said before she raised her hands, she was always raising her hands and she even hurt me and beat me hard and Jesus knows how hard she beat me because Jesus knows everything, he knows like Mama said before . . .

What was that thud at the door? After I turned off the light, because Jesus doesn't want me to stay awake when it's night because then the moths come and the bad thoughts, and I only went outside because I had to pee, and then I saw the girl and I just wanted to tell her that I wouldn't bother her anymore and she got scared and started running and I tried to run after her, Jesus knows I tried to run because I wanted to tell her that I wouldn't bother her anymore like he told me, Sandro—who played with the ball when he was a little boy and I said to him, "Sandro, will you throw me the ball?"—the son of Giancarlone who cares about me and gives me a house and feeds me and gives me work because otherwise, with that big, rotten, ugly head of mine, like Mama said before she raised her hands, she was always raising her hands, but now I have to open the door because that thud was a stone and if they throw stones at my house, they'll knock it down and then he'll get mad, Giancarlone who cares about me and gives me a house and feeds me and gives me work because otherwise, with that big, rotten, ugly head of mine, I open the door and look outside and there's no one there and what's this thing attached to the rock here at the door?

Oh, what a pretty little necklace, I wonder who gave it to me, I'll keep the necklace, because Jesus likes gifts, and it's a beautiful gift and will make Mama happy before she raises her hands, she was always raising her hands because I always made a mess, like when I was playing cards and knocked over the glasses because otherwise I drew my card too slowly and then it wasn't worth playing Briscola that way, and what a pretty necklace with a little turtle on it.

Six

The guy who was Polish, or whatever, pulled his dick out right in the middle of the little private show that Sandro had treated them all to, prompting Roman to give him a couple of slaps, as soon as the brunette, who was doing an interesting trick with the prosecco bottle, leaped to her feet saying, "You don't touch, got it?"

Sandro had arranged for a couple of private rooms for his boys. He knew the manager of Gilda's, Arturo. He was one of his father's boar-hunting buddies, with whom Giancarlo was doing some land deal. And to forget Fabiana, Sandro had pulled out his last hundred-euro note and granted himself twenty minutes in the company of two girls who twisted their tongues over every inch of his body. Still, the idea that Cedro was probably enjoying the beach and Fabiana continued to rile him, so much so that he was thinking of leaving and taking a ride over there to see if he spotted them.

He felt macho. Like his father. The talking-to he had given the Half-Wit that morning helped him feel that way. He had taken him aside, just as Giancarlo would have.

"I'm only going to tell you once, you filthy shitty pervert douche-bag," he'd said to him. "You look at my sister again, go near her again, and I'll cut off that little prick of yours with the gardening shears you use on the hedge. You get me? And then I'll stuff it in your mouth and make you chew it like gum. Understand? I'm not kidding, see. I'll even make you blow bubbles with it, like a piece of bubble gum, you hear me? Look, the only reason I'm not telling Giancarlo is because I want to be the one to hurt you if you do something like that again. Do you understand, you piece of shit?"

The Half-Wit hadn't breathed a word. All he did was nod, so vigorously that he seemed to be having a seizure. Sandro watched, feeling no pity for the guy. Should he have? Maybe. When he was little, the Half-Wit always tossed him the ball and then he'd say, "Sandro, will you throw me the ball?" Always just like that. And when little Sandro threw it to him, sending it into the hedge, the Half-Wit raised his arms as if the boy had scored a goal, then ran to him and picked him up to celebrate. Sandro remembered it clearly: when he was left alone in front of the house, he'd see that funny guy who looked like a panting gorilla coming, and he threw him the ball and then made him laugh. He always wore that light-blue cap with his hair sticking out at the sides like a clown. But now none of that feeling remained.

No hesitation. No soft spot.

Alice had asked him for help, not his father. And damn if that didn't make him feel awesome. Maybe Fabiana still thought he was an asshole like all the others, but those who knew him well, like his sister, knew that he was a guy with a nice pair of brass balls. And maybe now he'd go to the beach by himself and take a swim, and if Fabiana were around he would seem like a loner, which really melts the girls' hearts, even more than croissants with quiet music and the crap you say at certain moments, which seems like something out of a Laura Pausini song. What the fuck.

He made up his mind.

He allowed himself to relish the last few minutes of the *privé*, abandoning himself to the licking and stroking of the two girls who, upon seeing how much the client had shelled out for himself and all his friends, had evidently received clear instructions to give him a little extra.

When he left the private room at the end of his own little show, Sandro ordered a coffee at the bar and waited for the others.

"So you took the guys on an outing," Arturo said, coming up to him.

"It seems if they see a little pussy now and then, they work better."

"Bravo, Sandrino, you know what it takes."

"That goes for all of us, right?"

"The construction is moving along? Giancarlo is happy?"

"It's going okay."

"He had me by the balls over that thing. You know about it, right?"

"I don't know what you mean." But he knew all about it. A small piece of land, which for Arturo had not been buildable, had become so for Giancarlo right after he'd bought it from him.

"Between friends, playing tricks like that, there's no cause for it."

Sandro smiled broadly, an excuse to show his teeth. He took the pack of cigarettes out of the pocket of his leather jacket and lit one, which, given that smoking wasn't permitted, was like a dog taking a piss to mark his territory, telling you, "Careful, buddy. Don't go any farther."

"No tricks, Arturo. It's business. Learning to exploit situations is a skill that brings rewards. That eats at you?"

Arturo sniffs the piss. He doesn't go any farther. He seemed about to say something else, but then he picked up the phone and read something on the display.

"Excuse me, we'll talk more later," he said and walked away, holding the phone to his ear.

The guys were starting to head out. Roman came over.

"Great evening, Sandro. They had a good time. But the kid couldn't control himself, he made a mess in his pants and now he's in the bathroom washing up."

They saw him come out after a few minutes. He was drying himself off with toilet paper and laughing. A real jerk-off. In the parking lot Sandro waited until they were all in the van, then he slammed the door shut and got into his car.

He was already thinking about the beach, about the salty smell of the sea and the swim he'd decided to take, when he realized that his phone had slipped out of his pocket. He retrieved it under his feet and saw that there were a few missed calls and some messages.

He had set it on mute.

The messages were from the cell phone used to take reservations when the restaurant was closed.

He read the first message.

Call me. A

That *A* stood for Alice. Clearly, she had taken the wrong phone. Wasn't she with the Roman city boy? Had something happened?

There were five missed calls. All from that number.

Sandro immediately tried to call back. No answer. Another text told him he had a voice mail message. He tapped the number to listen to it.

Alice's voice sliced through like a razor.

"Where the hell are you, Sandro? I'm walking back and that fucking maniac is following me." Alice was breathing hard, she was running. Sandro looked around. How long had it been since the call? Shit. "Call me back, otherwise I'll have to call home, and if *he* comes he'll kill him and I don't want to talk to him about this. Come on, Sandro, call me. I'm almost to the road near the bend."

He tried to call again. But there was no answer, it just rang.

It had been more than three hours since the first unanswered call.

Sandro sped off in a rush toward the bend. It wasn't far from home. He kept calling that number. He also tried to call Alice's phone, but it must have been turned off.

"That shitty freak." He swore out loud, to fill the suffocating silence left by the unanswered calls. "If he did it again, this time I'm gonna hurt him. Fuck it. You didn't listen to me? Wasn't it enough, what I told you? Son of a bitch!" A fist on the dashboard. The phone again. More ringing. "What the fuck, Ali, answer me yourself! Fucking shit!" Ringing and ringing. "He didn't give a fuck. I told him something and he didn't give a fuck. Can you believe it?" The phone. No answer. "I'm going to beat that guy to a pulp." Ringing. "Fuck, Ali, answer the shitty phone, for shit's sake!"

More ringing.

He was driving at breakneck speed now. He narrowly avoided another car that appeared around a curve. He heard the prolonged sound of the horn as the other car passed.

"Fuck you too, asshole, and if you come by again later, I'll take that fucking car and shove it up your ass!"

Phone in his left hand, the other hand on the gearshift, the same number, ringing and ringing.

"Ali, I swear this time I'll make you look like a shit, you won't forget it, goddammit. Answer the phone, bitch!"

He reached the bend. Rolled down the window.

"Ali!"

The road was narrow and he couldn't leave the car on a curve. A short distance away there was a good spot to pull off into the trees. He brought the car to a stop, turned off the ignition, and stepped out into the woods.

"Ali!" he yelled, looking around. "Aliii!" There was no answer. Alice was no longer there. Maybe she made it home.

"What the fuck, Ali, the hell you could have answered!" he said, calling the house number from the contacts list.

"Hello?" His father's voice.

"It's me. Is Alice home?"

"How the hell do I know? What time is it, Sandro? What's happened?"

"Nothing, she'd called me, but I had the phone on mute. She was in some trouble, but she probably worked it out. Look and see if she's home, would you?"

And that's the end of it, he thought. *She's there, sleeping, and doesn't even realize the scare she gave me. She's always doing that, she never thinks about the consequences, that maybe someone will worry. She put the phone on mute and fell asleep, my brainy sister. She must have gotten the idiotic urge to take one of her nighttime walks listening to music in her earbuds. She can't just go and have fun like everyone else, not her. Too easy. She has to do these intellectual things. Shit, that way she can remind everyone that she has a humanities degree, she's not some jerk like this asshole here, running around in circles with a fucking phone in his hand looking for her all night, and now I don't even feel like going to the beach anymore to look for Fabiana, and for sure that bitch has already taken him into her mouth, that piece of shit Cedro who . . .*

"Sandro." His father again.

"Is she there?"

"No."

What does that mean?

"She's not home?"

"No, she's not here. What the hell happened? Do you mind telling me?"

"Could she be in the bathroom maybe?"

"Sandro, Alice isn't here. Tell me what the hell happened."

He looked around again. The woods. Maybe she went another way.

"I don't know, she called me but I had the phone on mute and didn't hear it."

"And you don't know what she wanted?"

"There was . . . I don't know, I told you, maybe . . ."

"Sandro, are you drunk or what? Did you take something?"

"I didn't take anything."

"So then for Chrissake will you tell me what the hell is going on?"

"The Half-Wit was there."

"What do you mean?"

"The Half-Wit was there bothering her. I told him to stop, but clearly that asshole didn't listen to me. Now when I find him, I'll fix him but good, you'll see."

"Wait there for me."

Giancarlo hung up.

Does he think I'm not capable of taking care of him by myself? I'll show him.

Sandro went into the woods to see if Alice had gone another way. Maybe she hadn't heard him. Maybe she was afraid and was hiding.

A fair amount of light filtered through the trees and you could see well enough in that area where the vegetation wasn't too dense.

"Ali, are you here?" he called. He kept phoning. Ringing and ringing. "Okay, you bastard." He started walking in the direction of the cabin where the Half-Wit lived. "That douchebag is going to have a bad night." Sandro was looking around when he spotted something.

It was on the ground. It looked like a big sack. Soiled—but not enough to prevent him from recognizing Alice's pale-blue blouse.

Seven

Giancarlo closed the bedroom door behind him without even waking his wife. She was sunk in a deep sleep induced by the vodka and antidepressants with which she marked her evenings spent in front of the television. All that remained of the woman he married was a black-and-white photograph from their wedding day. In it she was smiling. Then something strange had taken hold and consumed her over the years, leaving her there, comatose.

He hadn't liked the sound of Sandro's voice. He sensed trouble. He put a pod in the coffeemaker and made himself an espresso just to get his mouth ready for the first cigarette of the day. Outside it was still dark.

He stopped by the garage to get some things. The handheld spotlight he used for catching poachers and wild boar at night. The studded bat to rearrange the features of anyone who had dared bother his daughter. The rifle with boar-hunting buckshot should that someone be quick enough to escape the club.

He started the truck and, with a swift maneuver, turned down the provincial road to find Alice. That girl had filled her head with too many foolish ideas and showed no signs of improving. If she had spent half the time she'd wasted on books looking for a boyfriend, other than that moron who played around at being an artist with his parents' money, she would have had something to show for it at this point and wouldn't be lost in the middle of the night. Now he'd probably find her smoking somewhere with that music for depressed lunatics stuck in her ears. People who don't know their place sooner or later always end up in a jam. He had worked his ass off to build the family business, and now here he was sharing a cold bed with a human wreck and two ungrateful kids who, when you asked them to do something, it was like pulling teeth. He lit another cigarette.

The stretch of the provincial road he was on was dark. A whole bunch of assholes had decided that there should be no lights because of some kind of fucking bird that otherwise wouldn't stop here and would go and do its fucking business somewhere else. The restaurant hadn't been able to install a neon sign either and that pissed him off like you wouldn't believe. But sooner or later the tide would turn. Even those hypocritical environmentalists, who never missed a chance to hassle somebody else and then at home lit up their pool parties like daylight, would sooner or later stop calling the shots and fucking with people. And then the permit for his swimming pool would be issued, along with those for the bungalows and the outdoor picnic area with the grill and wood oven. And if any environmentalists got too close at that point, the boar-hunting buckshot was there ready to welcome them. Because they had to understand that it was his land and no one else's, and every man should be the master of his domain and be able to do what he wants.

He switched on the spotlight with one hand and aimed it into the woods as he drove. Usually there was someone beside him who handled the light when they went hunting for wild boars.

He felt the familiar gastric reflux in his throat. The coffee and cigarettes had stirred up his stomach. He opened the glove compartment and looked for the magnesia tablets he always carried with him.

"Now just calm down," he said to himself, "because with these nerves, if I catch someone, I'll shoot him for real."

He chewed the pill. As the stomach acids receded, he decided that as soon as this problem was dealt with, he would allow himself a visit to Sun Li—the Chinese girl in Case Basse—and get a nice full-body massage with hands and mouth that would fix him up right.

He reached the bend. A little farther on, with the spotlight, he was able to pick out Sandro's car among the trees. He pulled up behind it and climbed out of the pickup. With the gun slung over his shoulder, the bat in one hand, and the spotlight in the other, he approached his son's car and peered inside, examining everything closely. It was a bit of a mess, but he didn't see anything that looked like drugs.

"Sandro!" he called. Where the hell was that asshole?

The spotlight's large cone of light bobbed through the trees, illuminating branches and bushes.

"Sandro!"

He hooked the bat to the clip on his belt and got out his phone. He called Sandro's number. No answer. He called Alice's phone. Off. A fine pair of idiots. If he'd needed anything, he'd be better off calling Roman or Sun Li rather than his kids or, worse yet, what was left of his wife. If it was up to them, he could drop dead of a stroke out here and not be found for days.

"Sandro!" he called again.

He began walking, moving through the trees, with no clear idea of where he was going. Actually, he knew that forest as if it were his own living room. Alice and Alessandro, however, weren't like him, and at that hour, they would surely have gotten lost. And maybe that's just what had happened.

The sphere of white light moved slowly through the trees, preceding the practiced steps of the hunter. The night enveloped everything and every sound seemed muffled by the darkness—until a thud ricocheted across the woods and reached Giancarlo's ears. The white sphere jumped back and forth, like the eyes of an animal on alert.

"Alessandro, is that you?"

Another noise, similar to the first. Something being bashed. And then a scream.

Giancarlo pointed the light in the direction from which the scream had come. A male voice. A cry of pain, something terrible. He started running toward it. He knew the Half-Wit's cabin was over that way.

"The Half-Wit was bothering her," Sandro had said.

Alice.

Eight

The white brilliance of the spotlight. A tangle of trees and bushes. And, finally, the beam reached Sandro, motionless in front of the small cabin. The wild-eyed stare of a wounded beast.

When Giancarlo approached and shone the light on his son, he saw that he was holding a shovel, covered with something that looked like soil.

However, when Giancarlo looked closer, he realized that it was not soil.

"What the hell happened?" he shouted. Sandro didn't answer. He just stared at him, still sunk in an abyss. Giancarlo went over to the cabin. It was all smashed up. It looked like a cyclone had hit it. "Either you tell me what the hell happened or . . ."

And then he saw it.

The Half-Wit's body was lying on the ground outside the cabin door. Giancarlo went over to it. The Half-Wit's head was no longer recognizable. It was shattered, like a vase dropped on the floor. The ogre's sick brain was smeared on the ground around what remained of his skull. A mushy puddle.

"The Half-Wit was there bothering her."

At first it was just a feeling. Something dark and cruel rose in him, slinking in the shadows, feeding on his ever-rising fear, as that shapeless thing crept into his mind, whispering his daughter's name. Then that feeling became a vise, a clawed hand that gripped his chest and began squeezing his heart, as if to drain away every drop of blood inside him. He fell to his knees beside the Half-Wit's lifeless body.

"Why don't you say something, Sandro?" He hardly even recognized his own voice, which for the first time seemed so frail, keening like that of a child. "What did you do?" He felt dizzy as if he might black out. Even hoped he would. But he didn't. At the same time, he felt heavy, like he was made of stone. He couldn't get up. There were flies buzzing around the Half-Wit's smashed cranium.

"Sandro . . ." He breathed in as much air as he needed for that thin little voice and ripped out the monster that was gnawing at his heart. "Where is Alice?"

His son finally saw him. Sandro's gaze fell on his father, an unnatural wonder in his eyes, as if he were seeing him for the first time.

"Sandro," Giancarlo said again, pleading. "Where is my little girl?"

Nine

And that's how Giancarlo Bastiani, my father, took responsibility that night for a murder he did not commit.

When he finally found my body, all the strength left him and he slumped to the ground. Grief twisted his face into a mute grimace. He cradled my cold head in his hands, stroking my hair as he'd done when I was small enough to fit in the crook of his arm.

My skull was cracked open on the left side of my face. My blood was already dry, my hair moist and sticky. For a moment the anguish was so intense that my father must have thought of ending it all with a rifle shot in the mouth. His muscles were numb with tension, his hands could have crushed a rock. He dug his fingers into the earth with such force that he broke his fingernails. I think it was because of my brother that he struggled to regain what little lucidity he needed to fix what could still be fixed. And the only thing he could still do for his children was to keep Alessandro from being arrested and charged. My father had known prison as a young man. It was one of those things that he did not like to talk about, but once he had beaten a guy who had made him see red, as he put it. He had spent several months inside. Sandro, however, would end up in jail for a good part of his life for what he had done to the Half-Wit. And his son, as much as he tried to appear strong, wasn't anything like him. I don't know how he thought of all the rest.

Sandro crouched beside him now. He was holding my necklace with the turtle pendant, Mr. Toby. He told my father about the Half-Wit. He told him that I had asked him to protect me and that he had failed me. He told him about the phone call that I had made, that he hadn't heard. About the text message I'd left him when the Half-Wit started running after me. He told him that he had found the Half-Wit standing in front of the cabin with my necklace in his hand. And that when he'd asked him what he had done to his sister, the freak had started saying that he hadn't meant to hurt her, that he hadn't meant to scare her, that he hadn't meant to make her run away, that he had started running after her to tell her that he wouldn't bother her anymore, that he'd really wanted to tell her that, but that she kept running and he didn't know what to do, and he hadn't even been able to finish telling him before Sandro had already stunned him with the first whack of the shovel that he'd found in his hand. God only knew how hard he had brought it down on that monster.

But now he spoke about it as if it concerned someone else, with a wide-eyed stare, still trapped in the abyss into which he had plunged.

My father told him to go home. To take a shower and clean himself up. To wait for Marshal Torrese to come and get him, and then to tell him that something terrible had happened. To pretend he knew nothing about it. Focus, and he might manage to pull it off. My father said he knew how difficult it would be, but that *by God!* (that's just what he said) he was going to make sure he didn't lose his son as well. So Sandro, who was not yet fully aware of what was going on, his eyes still haunted, went home.

My father gently laid my head on a cushion of leaves. He braced himself and went to get the shovel that my brother had used to slaughter the Half-Wit. He wiped the handle off on his shirt and then, holding it tightly in one hand, dealt a couple of blows to what remained of the skull that my brother had staved in. He brought it down with such force that his face and shirt were splattered with blood. Finally, he took

his rifle and shot the Half-Wit in the neck. Then he stood there looking at what was left of that big hulking brute whom he had kept with
him for as long as he could remember, like you do with a beat-up dog
found on the street.

He set the rifle and shovel on the ground. He lit a cigarette and sat
down next to my body. He stroked my face with a gentleness that he
had never shown. And he went on like that, waiting for enough time to
pass to allow Sandro to get home safely. Then he picked up the phone
and punched in Torrese's number.

He told him that I had not returned home and that he'd been worried. He had looked for me just about everywhere and then he'd remembered that the Half-Wit had bothered me on a couple of occasions. And
so he'd found my body and realized what must have happened. He'd
gone to the Half-Wit's cabin and found him there out front, with my
necklace still in his hand, and he had confessed everything to him.

The rest is not so hard to imagine.

I had been killed with a rock. There were still shards in my skull.
But the rock was not found. No one ever found the phone from which
I had called my brother either. My father's story held together, and in
the course of the investigation that followed, every element seemed to
confirm it. He got twenty years. The judge considered his emotional
state, but also the savagery of the crime. There was no appeal. His lawyer
didn't understand why, but my father preferred to end it that way. His
body, however, stopped functioning and a heart attack killed him a few
years later, shortly after he'd requested house arrest in order to take care
of himself. He never breathed a word about it to anyone.

Sandro went home that night and did everything that our father
had told him to do. He took a shower, clothes and all, and let the blood
and soil run off him. Then he undressed, finished washing, stuffed the
wet clothes in a bag, and threw them out along with the restaurant's
garbage. He checked to make sure that his mother was still asleep,
then crawled into bed and lay there waiting. He was exhausted all of a

sudden, as if he had one of those high fevers that knock you out and leave you half senseless, alternately shivering and sweating. An unnatural sleep came over him. He was haunted by the sole thought of that phone call. Of how things would have turned out if he had only heard it and had responded in time. He kept picturing the scene. That night, right in the middle of his own private little show, the phone rings, he answers and hears my voice, I explain it all to him, and he speeds off and comes to get me and finds me there waiting for him on the side of the road, and I smile at him when I see him coming and climb into the car, and we laugh and laugh all the way home. We're not sleepy, so we go into the kitchen and eat ice cream like we used to do when we were little.

But each time the shivers racked his body, he would open his eyes and I wasn't there. And he found himself back in that reality in which he had not heard my call, but instead had found me dead in the woods, had killed the Half-Wit, slaughtering him with a shovel, and then had left my father to clean up the whole mess. More shivers, more jerking awake. Until the doorbell rang.

When he stood up, he felt weak. His legs heavy, achy, and limp. He didn't think he could even walk straight. Maybe he really did have a fever.

He opened the door and found himself face-to-face with Torrese.

The police took him to the spot where my body had been found. They told him about his father, who was at the station, that they'd had to give him a sedative because he wasn't feeling so good.

"Not feeling so good." That's just what they said.

When he saw the white sheet in the woods, his legs buckled. He slumped to the ground, not far from my body. Sandro remained there, while around him pretty much the whole town began to gather. Only when he saw Enrico coming did he find the strength to get up. He remembered that I was supposed to be with him. He went over to him. He really just wanted to ask him how I had ended up alone. But he still wasn't able to fully control his body. Just as his legs still wobbled and couldn't support him, so his voice came and went between sobs and moments when breath seemed to fail him altogether.

He spewed it all out angrily and, as he did, he brought up more rage looking for a way out; he found he felt better when he was able to puke it up. So he leaned against a tree to recover a bit, and as soon as he felt ready, he lunged at Enrico, shouting at him.

The police stopped him and took him aside. They let him get it out of his system. Marshal Torrese stared at Enrico strangely.

That's what happened that evening. My brother would carry with him the truth about the Half-Wit's death, as our father had told him to. He never breathed a word to anyone.

When he buried my father, a few years later, he was alone in the cemetery. My mother had already entered an artificial world of psycho-tropic drugs that kept her from ever leaving the house.

When he left the cemetery, the truth that no one else would ever know felt even heavier inside him. That his father, Giancarlo Bastiani, was not a murderer. That his father, that monstrous night, to spare his son from the horrible act that he had committed, had assumed a guilt that was not his. What not even Sandro could have imagined was that his father was not the only one to have done so. Except that the Half-Wit had not decided, of his own volition, to cover up for a killer.

PART THREE

MR. TOBY

One

The Euronics poster with discounted prices for computers, tablets, mobile phones, and microwave ovens is the most recent one she finds. Then there's the one with the cream that helps eradicate wrinkles, the one for the yogurt that helps you poop, and the one for the insurance company that shows elderly people happy and smiling on a perpetual vacation somewhere that seems light-years away from here. Chiara finds them every morning, under the shelter where she waits for the bus that takes her to school. Backpack resting on the ground between her legs, jacket zipped up to her chin, hands in her pockets, the hood under which there must be a face but from which only two white cables stick out, carrying the voice of Chris Martin of Coldplay into her head, a song that says something about Jerusalem bells.

Now and then she imagines that someday a different bus than usual will pull up. A white bus with tinted windowpanes, the kind that don't allow you to see in. It will stop in front of her and the door will open, and inside there'll be a suite or something, with a Jacuzzi tub and a tray of chocolates and strawberries and a bottle of sparkling Brachetto. The best thing is that there will be no one inside, and she can go traveling to the most beautiful cities in the world inside her whirlpool tub whose water is always hot. One day she will pass through London to pick up Margherita and take her along for a ride. They can take a picture together in the foaming bath bubbles, holding the Brachetto, and post it on Facebook with a very simple four-word message, meant for everyone.

Adios and fuck you.

That bus, however, never comes. And after she lets herself be lulled for a while by the fantasy, it's always the blue Tiemme bus that pulls up and opens its door to her. Inside it's always very hot. If she's by herself, she sits as far from the other passengers as possible, and leans her head against the window, dozing for ten minutes or so. But if Valentina is there, they chat a bit. Sometimes Valentina goes with her brother, though, so she isn't always on the bus. This morning she is.

"Over here, Kia," she says, sliding over to the seat next to the window.

"Ciao, Vale." Chiara sits down and takes out an earbud.

"So, tell me, how was dinner with that guy last night? Did they talk about that girl?"

"They said something, yeah, but mostly a bunch of things that had nothing to do with her."

"A big bore then."

"They mentioned her a couple of times, that's it. They didn't say a word about her being killed by that maniac."

"Have you told your grandmother?"

"Think I should I call her?"

"I don't know, Kia. What do you think?"

"She'd want me to call her."

"Then maybe she'd ask you to come and see her, and then we can do some more shopping at Castel Romano."

"I have an idea she would pay a lot to know about last night."

"You answered your own question."

"I'll text her later in class. This morning I really don't have the head to focus."

"Kia, this morning you won't have to."

"Meaning?"

"Rigoni is giving the class a pop quiz, in history."

"Shit."

"She told us yesterday."

"Yesterday I didn't get there until second period, Vale. What the fuck? You could have told me."

"Shit."

"Shit and more shit."

"How far along are you?"

"Like I haven't opened my history book since last month."

"Not good, Kia."

"Yeah. Bad."

"She'll flunk you."

"She's not even going to see me this morning."

"You know how pissed off she gets if you skip class."

"Anyway, tomorrow is Sunday. I'll stay home and catch up."

"Sure."

"Can you tell her we talked last night and I had a slight fever?"

"No way, that woman will take aim at me."

"Come on, Vale, tell her at the end of class."

"At the end of class if it seems right, but I can't guarantee anything."

Chiara looks out the window. Soon the bus will stop on the provincial road. All she has to do is get off and walk about ten minutes to get to a dirt road and from there it's easy. No cars pass by there, no one will catch her. The dirt road leads to the coast highway. Just cross it and you're on the beach. A walk up to the Miramare and she can make herself comfortable behind the beach club, which is closed, and maybe she can start her total immersion in history there, that way part of Sunday will be spared.

"I'm disappearing," she tells Valentina.

"Good luck."

The bus stops. Chiara goes to the back. Gets off. When the bus pulls away, she is alone on the provincial road. This is the riskiest stretch because cars go by here and someone might spot her. But at this moment there's no one. And it's a beautiful sunny morning, without so much as a cloud in the sky. A pleasant warm breeze brushes her face. It's the most exciting moment of the day, when everything still lies ahead. She pulls her hood over her head. She leaves one ear free so she can hear any cars that might approach. In the other ear Coldplay performs "Death and All His Friends." She starts walking.

Two

The sun is really warm. It's a pleasure to lie there on her coat, spread out under her like a towel, a few steps from the sea. A couple of cigarette butts stuck in the sand, earbuds with Chris's voice, the smell of salt air, the backpack cradling her head, and the open history book propped on her chest so as not to feel too guilty.

Along the road everything went smoothly: just a few cars passed by, but Chiara had time to duck behind the guardrail. She came to the dirt road and from there it was a peaceful walk. She crossed the coast road to the beach. She walked a little way, and as soon as she reached the Miramare, she settled behind the bathhouse and opened the history book. In the shade, though, it was a little chilly, so she moved onto the sand, letting all her good intentions melt away in the sun like a cherry Popsicle.

Too bad she can't write anything on Facebook, because it would be good to make the others a little envious; though being the jealous little shits they are, they would probably expose her in no time. Too bad, she knew exactly what she would write if she could: since she couldn't say "adios" yet, she would simply say "fuck you." She did take a selfie on the beach with the predictable Converse All Stars prominently featured, however, and sooner or later she'll find a way to share it with a small circle of people. With Margherita, maybe. But who knows if she's already crossed over to the other side and would rat her out.

I get you, big sis. I mean, even if it were somewhat true what they say, that you went a little nuts. Look, it's not the end of the world. Hey, it shows that you're normal, because a person would really have to be crazy to want to stay around here. Okay, there's the sea, and the beach this morning is gorgeous, but you can find the sea and beautiful beaches in a lot of places. Maybe someday I'd like to come back here again, sure. Come back and look at everything from the outside.

She checks the time on her iPhone: soon Valentina will send her a message telling her how things went with the blitz quiz, meaning three abrupt questions for each of them that's it. All questions that you could answer in a nanosecond if you had a smartphone, which goes to prove that learning the material by heart is totally useless. Maybe it's hard to determine how many gigabytes of space a person has in his brain, which for sure isn't the same for everyone, and just like smartphones there must be 16-gigabyte brains and brains with 32 gigabytes and 64 gigabytes and 128 gigabytes and so on, up to a terabyte, but in any case, regardless of how many there are, using them to store information that can instantly be found on Google is definitely not the way to go. Further proof, if it were needed, that high school is nothing but a huge waste of time. Adults, such as her mother, don't get it because they aren't "digital natives," as normal people like her generation are called. Yet they have the authority to ask you three shitty little questions and grade you based on how you answer. Rigoni, for that matter, with her old cell phone and its small buttons that light up, certainly isn't even capable of sending an e-mail. But then teachers are a particularly pathetic category, and at home Rigoni most likely has one of those old computers, which to boot up . . .

That's weird. It feels like a cloud has covered the sun. Yet there isn't a single one in the sky. She opens her eyes. It's not a cloud that's covering the sun. It's a person.

It takes her a few seconds to recognize him, as the dazzling effect diminishes and the profile silhouetted against the light is filled in with details that become features.

"Ciao," says Enrico, the guy who had dinner with her parents last night.

"Ciao."

"Alternate plan this morning?"

"Huh?"

"That's what we used to call it. Alternate plan."

"You won't tell my parents, will you?"

"Of course not."

Chiara is about to stand up, because it seems like a sensible thing to do, and go along with this guy who apparently, for the moment, is not about to get her in trouble. He, however, sits down on the sand, beside her jacket.

"If I had gone to school around here, I doubt that I would ever have been able to graduate."

"Why?"

"Because I would have ended up here every morning."

"In Rome it must not have been so bad. I mean, there must have been plenty of opportunities for your 'alternate plan.'"

"Oh sure, of course. I liked the Domus Aurea, near the Colosseum. It was good because of the metro stops. And nearby there was a kiosk that made focaccias stuffed with mortadella that had the taste of that forbidden holiday." He looks around. "Around here, though, everything is closed."

"Around here, everyone knows you and it would be dumb to get caught for a focaccia with mortadella, don't you think?"

"Sure, but there's another possibility."

The Veliero is open in the morning, because the home for the elderly brings its residents there to enjoy the sun and a cappuccino.

Apparently, Enrico has been wandering up and down the beach for some time.

A few minutes later, he comes back with a bag in his hand. They sit on the wooden steps of the Miramare and take out the pizza and two cans of Coke.

"Didn't they have beer?" Chiara asks.

"No, they only have things they serve the old people."

"I'll bet. Do you really think I don't drink beer?"

"At this hour?"

"What's wrong with that?"

"Okay, I owe you a beer."

The pizza, though, isn't bad. The tomato is sweet and the mozzarella is nice and melty, not like the kind that tastes like plastic because it's been sitting around too long. They eat in silence.

Now that she's not wearing the earbuds, Chiara can hear the sound of the waves. It's strange how after a while you don't even notice it anymore, but if you begin to focus on it, you can't help hearing it and eventually it becomes almost deafening. She considers sharing this thought, because it seems like the kind of thing that someone like Enrico might appreciate. She's about to tell him, but he breaks the silence first.

"You must have been bored last night."

"No, of course not."

"Don't be polite. I'd be bored in your place."

"Maybe, but just a little."

"You can say it. I promise that even if you were to say something wrong, I wouldn't tell your parents."

"Actually, more disappointed than bored." She realizes too late the implications of what she just said.

"Disappointed? By what?"

"No, nothing, it was just something to say. Actually, bored was more like it."

"You thought we would talk about Alice, right?"

Chiara would like to respond by changing the subject, but she can't. It's not like when they ask you a question at school and you don't know the answer and try to fudge it by talking about something else. Here she's finding it difficult to recover.

"There's nothing wrong with it, Chiara. It's normal for you to be curious. Everyone here is." He smiles at her and takes the last bite of his pizza. He wipes the greasy crumbs off his lips with one of the paper napkins he'd put in the bag. He picks up the can of Coke and takes a sip.

"You were little at the time. How old were you?"

"I was six years old. I was with Margherita that night, at my grandmother's."

"Steely Gloria."

"Steely."

"I don't think she ever cooked anything more complicated than toast, but she chauffeured us around everywhere. When your mother and I were kids, she took us to a Rolling Stones concert."

"Too bad my mother didn't take after her."

"So, you don't remember anything about that night? But you must have talked about it with your girlfriends, and you must have exchanged plenty of stories about what happened. So you most likely know everything, I imagine."

"More or less."

"Then why were you disappointed? What did you want to hear?" He turns to her, and this time it's as if he were cornering her, back to the wall, with those blue eyes. They are not aggressive eyes, though.

"I don't know. I just said it without thinking."

"You did, well, the best things are usually said that way. The problem, instead, is when you think about it too much, and then you don't say it but it shows on your face."

"And do they all do that with you?"

"Right."

"And that's why you never came back here?"

129

"Right again."

"I'm sorry."

"What for? You didn't do anything."

"Yes, I did. I mean, you buy me lunch, and I start talking to you about these things. I'm really sorry."

"I've wanted to come back here for a long time." He looks out at the sea again, as if loosening his hold. As if he were opening up and letting those words discreetly flow away. "You can't imagine how many times I left the house, got in the car, and started driving. But I always turned back. It was as if I lacked a plausible reason to come here. As if I didn't want to allow myself the right to need to come and that's that. One day I drove around the entire ring road twice before returning home, and I only went back because Giulia called me on the cell phone needing me to pick her up. Giulia is my fiancée. The truth is that if I had come back here sooner, maybe it might have been better."

"My parents mentioned you occasionally. But usually they avoid talking about what happened that night."

Enrico turns to her and waits for her to continue.

"Here in town everyone avoids talking about it. That's why everything here seems to have stopped since that day. People need to talk about what they're carrying inside them, at least that's how I see it."

"You don't know how right you are." Enrico smiles.

"They all act like nothing happened, until something comes up that reminds them of that night and then they lower their eyes, shake their heads, and change the subject."

"That's the way grown-ups deal with certain things."

"It's the wrong way."

"It's a way to make things disappear. It comes in handy when you yourself would like to disappear and can't."

"Would you like to disappear?"

Enrico thinks it over a bit before answering. "Let's say that at times it would all be easier, being able to."

130

"Still, it's a little like sweeping it under the rug."

"You think so?"

"Even if only for that girl, Alice. Last year a group, they're called the Speedballs, played at the high school dance and dedicated a song to Alice Bastiani. It was a number that Jeff Buckley sang, but I think someone else wrote it. 'Hallelujah' it's called, like those religious things. There were a lot of kids who didn't know who Alice Bastiani was. And when I told my parents, they thought it was normal that no one knew anything about it, and that in fact it was inappropriate to dedicate a song to her, because in the end it's something that happened a long time ago. It's that kind of attitude that I just don't get."

"Besides that, it's a beautiful song."

"Gorgeous."

"Anyway, the one who wrote it is Leonard Cohen."

"Does it bother you?"

"What?"

"That they dedicated a song to a girl who . . . I mean, Alice was your girlfriend, right?"

"Yeah, sure." He smiles. "And I think she would have liked the Speedballs."

"They're not that great, but they make a big racket and the singer isn't so bad."

"And Alice's brother, Sandro, do you know him?"

A question Chiara wasn't expecting. "He's a junkie. The hard stuff too. He's been in a lot of hot water, thefts and things like that. He lives in that house that's falling apart, with his mother. Apparently she doesn't leave her room anymore. She's a mess, no longer in her right mind."

"And him?"

"I don't know, is there something in particular you want to know?"

"I need to talk to him."

"That won't be difficult. You know the Fuorimano, the pub on the other side of the Aurelia?"

"Sure."

"He's usually there in the afternoon. He plays the slot machines, drinks one Campari after another, and waits for evening to shoot up. If you catch him soon, you'll be able to talk to him, later he starts getting too drunk."

They stay there a while longer. Chiara hands him an earbud, and they listen to a few Coldplay songs together as the sun gets even hotter. Unfortunately, there are no more cigarettes. Chris's voice, however, is interrupted by the arrival of a text. It's Valentina.

She slaughtered us.

Chiara realizes that it's twelve thirty. The message just arrived, maybe the phone was out of range.

"I think I'd better go."

"Isn't it too early for a student who went to school?"

"I have to go catch the bus to arrive home on time, and the bus stop is far away."

"I can't give you a ride. I came on foot."

"No problem."

Chiara gets up and puts on her jacket, but it's hot and she doesn't zip it up. She slings the backpack over one shoulder, waves good-bye, and starts walking. After a few steps, however, she turns to Enrico.

"Thanks for lunch."

"Sure."

"I think it would have been fun to be your girlfriend."

"You would have had a free pizza every morning."

Chiara smiles and continues walking. She knows Enrico may be following her with his eyes so she tries to walk properly, without dragging her feet as she usually does.

And she's right. Enrico watches her as she walks away. Usually he can never see any resemblance between parents and their children, but he thinks she seems to have something of Betti, although he couldn't say what exactly. He tries to enjoy the sun a little longer before going to look for Sandro. He has to do it. He has to find out if there are things he doesn't know, because there's still that question, which he never spoke about to anyone.

He remembers it so clearly; the sky was turning dark and there was the sound of that car door closing. A stupid argument. Alice had changed her mind and said she wouldn't go to live with him. Everything was all set, he'd wanted to tell her. That summer he had arrived a little late because he had found an apartment with a terrace, for outdoor suppers the way she liked it. He'd wanted to tell her about that. That, and a lot of other plans he'd come up with, trips and things they could do together. But something in her had changed and he didn't know what it was. Then the question that had popped out just like that, without his ever intending it: *Is there someone else?*

There was a time when he was actually certain of it. At other times, however, he'd had the impression that she was offended by the accusation, and had stormed out of the car for that reason. Eventually, though, he realized that the only real fact was that she had never answered the question. Should he have told someone? But who? That marshal who was itching to smash in his face because of some marijuana? And what would he have said?

He'd carried it with him, locked inside somewhere.

Was that what the message sent from Alice's number was referring to? Was that what he didn't know? Was there a chance that Alice had spoken to her brother about something like that?

Enrico was sure of one thing at least. This time he wasn't leaving without knowing all the answers.

Three

"I hope Rigoni kicks your ass Monday, because today you dodged something really hellacious."

On the bus Valentina slides over to the window to make room for Chiara, handing her an earbud so they can listen to the same song as they talk. Lana Del Rey welcomes her back with "Born to Die," which by now Valentina is categorically obsessed with. They wait for the end of the song in an almost liturgical silence, as its last mournful notes fade out.

"I met Enrico Sarti at the beach," Chiara says as soon as Vale's playlist moves on to the next selection, "Back to Black" by Amy Winehouse, which she isn't interested in hearing.

"The guy who was at your parents' for dinner last night?"

"Yeah, him. Alice's boyfriend."

"Did you talk about the murder?"

Amy starts singing, but Vale also seems more interested in other things.

"That too."

"Awesome!"

"Not so much."

"Meaning?"

"All in all, he's a normal guy with a huge guilt complex. He seemed sad more than anything else. But in a . . . how should I put it . . . sweet way."

"He's sad, in other words, sweet, there on the beach . . . Kia, did you fuck him?"

"What the hell are you saying?"

"Nothing, I just want to know, so I'll at least understand what follows better."

"No."

"Okay, okay, it was just to get the whole picture."

"There's nothing to get. We talked about a few things and we had lunch. That's all."

"Sure."

"You're hopeless."

"Not even a blow job?"

This time she can't help it and bursts out laughing. A woman with a somewhat weary look turns toward them. Her expression says "I really wish you would stop that," but that only makes it more fun.

Chiara gets off at her stop, like any normal day, and walks home, down the street with the little houses, one next to the other, each with a small garden and flower pots and a lawn and a doormat that says "WELCOME." When she arrives at her house, she sees her parents getting out of the car. They don't notice her. Her mother is walking swiftly, head down. She does that when she's really pissed off. Chiara hides behind a parked car. Her father follows Betti. He too seems all worked up. She's busted. They called the school and they know everything. Shit. Now what?

She approaches the house, trying to stay hidden behind the low wall. She hears the door slam and sees them in the kitchen. They're arguing. She has to know what they're saying. If they caught her, she'll call Valentina and disappear somewhere. Otherwise they'll keep her home all weekend, and she has to go out with Gibo tonight. She runs around the house and enters through the back gate. She reaches the French doors to the kitchen, but they're locked from the inside. She dashes back around the house to the front door. Her parents are a few steps away, but inside.

"Don't ever do that again," her father is saying. "I won't have you making a scene when I'm at work. If you have something to say to me, wait till I come home and tell me. You have to stop acting like a hysteric."

"Last night you still weren't home at four a.m. I took the pills because I had an anxiety attack, and this morning you weren't here. I tried calling you everywhere, but you didn't answer, and now you're telling me I shouldn't ask where the fuck you spent the night?"

"I came home and you were sleeping. I was with Enrico."

"You weren't with Enrico. Don't bullshit me."

Betti must be losing it to talk like that. The good news is that they're not talking about her and school. But she doesn't go in yet. She knows that if she opens the door, they will stop fighting, and she wants to know what's going on.

"Listen to me, Betti. You have to calm down. I was with Enrico and he told me something. So I had a few things to do. It's something important."

"What?"

"I brought him the stuff he had left at the house, remember? Among all those things was his phone. I didn't remember it, but he turned it on and saw that someone had sent him two messages after the funeral, from Alice's phone."

Silence.

Chiara does her best to squeeze between the front door and the kitchen window to avoid being seen.

"What does it mean?" her mother asks.

"That someone had Alice's phone."

"Alice's phone?"

"You heard me."

"How can that be?"

"I don't know."

"But is it the phone that . . ."

"That's the one, Betti."

"And someone found it?"

"Apparently."

"That's not possible, I . . ."

"Betti, it's true."

Silence.

"Who?"

"Sandro, maybe," her father says.

"Sandro?"

"The other day Enrico spotted someone in the garden, and before I got there I saw Sandro's car. When Enrico told me about the messages, I asked the security agency to increase the patrols to the area. And last night the security guard on duty caught Sandro in the car, spying on Enrico's house again. When he saw the guard, he drove off, but the guy got his license plate number."

Silence again. Chiara isn't able to see them from where she's crouched. But she hears the sound of a cabinet door opening, glasses, water running in the sink.

"Is Enrico worried?"

"I don't think so."

"Are you?"

"I'd just like to know what that junkie wants from him."

"You couldn't have been talking to the agency until four a.m."

"Actually, I took a little drive afterward. I needed to think. It's not so inconceivable that Enrico's return stirred things up for me a bit, is it?"

"You think you're the only one?"

"No, but that makes no difference."

Silence. Chiara is still holding her breath.

"I'll start the water for the pasta," Betti says. "Chiara will be home any minute. Let's try to calm down."

The clatter of dishes, tap water running into the pot, drawers and cabinet doors slamming, cutlery brought to the table. They don't say anything more. Chiara opens the door.

"Be right there," she says, running up the stairs.

"The pasta will be ready in fifteen minutes!" her mother shouts after her.

Chiara goes to her room and shuts the door behind her. She grabs her iPhone and brings up WhatsApp to send a message to Margherita.

Ciao, Marghe, you're missing something. Enrico Sarti, the guy Alice was going with, is back in town. I think he's here to sell the house or something like that. This morning I met him on the beach and we talked. He's a nice guy, we had lunch together.

Maybe it's best to leave out the part about the beach for now. She deletes the last two sentences and begins again.

It seems that Sandro, Alice's brother, is spying on him. They caught him around his house a few times. Apparently, it has to do with a couple of messages that Enrico received from Alice's phone after she died. I heard the old folks talking about it. They don't know I heard them. It sounds as if Sandro wants something.

And this morning when she met Enrico, he in fact asked her about Sandro. Those two will meet and something will happen, but that's more complicated to write because of the beach where she shouldn't have been.

The old fogeys seem very worried. If you ask me, there's something serious going on. Gotta go now, Mom is already freaking out as it is over this thing, and if the pasta gets cold on the table, it's the end of the world. I'll keep you posted. I feel like I'm in that DVD series you let me watch, remember? The one with the girl they find dead on the shore and then that guy comes to town and investigates?

She brings up Google because she can't remember the title. The girl's name was Laura Palmer. Found it.

Twin Peaks, remember? The guy who in the end was a demon who took possession of people and controlled them and made them do all those things . . . As soon as a dwarf who speaks backward appears, I'll let you know. XXX.

She goes downstairs. Her parents are in the kitchen. They smile at her. The pasta is on the table, and the whole scene reminds her of one of those commercials where the family is smiling happily around a bowl of steaming pasta, which the mother places on the table, and everyone looks on, excited, as if they hadn't eaten for a month.

"How was school this morning?" Betti asks.

"The usual."

But she has the feeling that if she had told them a classmate had pulled out a bazooka and staged a massacre, the effect would have been the same. Her parents seem distracted. Usually when her mother, who is the weird one, acts like that, she and her father look at each other and laugh. But this time it's different. He too seems worried. Something's wrong in the pasta commercial.

"So then," Betti asks again, "how was school this morning?"

Something is definitely wrong.

Four

There are three rows, each composed of five slots that fill from time to time with oranges, pineapples, cherries, watermelons, and various colored letters. The crushed fruit is the joker and doubles each time someone wins. The farmer is the only figure that moves, and he has a shit-eating grin that makes you want to stick him in a filthy toilet and flush him down, just to wipe away that asshole smile. There are numerous winning combinations, but for Sandro Bastiani, the only victory is when, with twenty euros worth of tokens, he is able to pass the time with some Campari and a couple of cigarettes.

The dirty ashtray is sitting on the machine, the glass next to it. His hands move over the keys to decide on what to bet and choose which slots to keep and which to spin. His fingernails are black, and if his hands stay still too long, they start to shake. The heroin craving starts in the early afternoon, not long after his coffee, but it's too early. The nightmares have to be kept at bay for a while longer. He has to wait a few more hours in order to spend a quiet night. Otherwise he will need another ride on the merry-go-round to face the night, and his supply is running out and won't be replenished until Tuesday. Twenty euros worth of tokens, ten euros to cover three Camparis and a bag of peanuts, he has cigarettes for tonight, and all he has to do is wait for the hours to slip away as painlessly as possible until it's time to shoot up.

Perched on the stool in front of the slot machine, Sandro resembles a scarecrow. He's wearing a tight black leather jacket, to protect him from a cold that comes from within and doesn't let up. Filthy jeans that are now too big for what's left of him. Shoes untied because of the tormenting pain in his feet.

He tries to stay far enough away from the luminous screen so as not to spot his reflection, because every time he sees it, it scares him. He's a bad X-ray of Alessandro as he used to be, of whom nothing remains but some expired leftovers.

The room with the slot machines is a small space with yellowish, smoke-filmed walls and the indelible stench of sour sweat. There is a door leading to the back that lets the cold in, along with the continuous smack of a deflated ball thrown against a wall by a boy who has nothing else to do, and the afternoon light that has begun to turn orange.

Tonight there are some additional worries to chase off with oranges, pineapples, cherries, watermelons, and various colored letters that revolve and spin away. Enrico Sarti is back and Sandro wants to see how he is. Whether time had destroyed him too, or whether the only one left shattered is the inveterate, psychedelic gambler of Happy Farm here.

Three smiling pineapples reload some credits. The farmer cheers, waving his straw hat and pitchfork. The boy's ball keeps slamming against the wall, the cold creeps in, the Campari is finished, and all that remains is the orange slice to suck on, as the farm's merry little tune funnels away the minutes, one after the other.

But the finale comes soon. And it's unexpected. It appears behind him, gliding through the door silently, the way ghosts always do.

"Hello, Sandro."

Enrico has found him.

The last slot is still spinning—with a cherry, three of a kind would recharge some credits—but it's no use: just a watermelon. The farmer's face is aggrieved, the button for the stakes and the one to activate the slots begin flashing in turn.

"What do you want?" Not even turning around.

"I should ask you the same question, don't you think?"

"I wanted to see how you looked."

"That's all?"

No. That's not all.

"You're doing well, I see, Mr. Architect. Not me. You must know that. So, good for you."

"Isn't there anything else you want to tell me?"

The dirty fingers of the inveterate, psychedelic gambler of Happy Farm stop. Before his hands start to shake, Sandro puts them in his pockets and rotates on the stool to face Enrico.

"What the hell should I have to tell you? Let's hear it."

"You came to my house to spy on me. The other night they found you in the car in front of my house again. I'm leaving, Sandro. I'm selling everything. I only came back so I could leave for good."

"Bravo, leave it all behind and have a good life."

"Blaming me didn't help you to live your own better."

"What the fuck do you know? Huh? You come back here after ten years and you want to talk? What do you want to hear? That nobody holds it against you for what happened to my sister? Fine, get the fuck out. You made a new life for yourself and you did well. It wasn't your family after all, it was mine."

"Why did you send me those messages, after the funeral?"

"I don't know what you're talking about."

"You wrote that there were things I didn't know."

"I didn't send you any messages."

"I only saw them now. They were in the phone memory. You could have found another way to contact me if you had something to tell me."

"What the fuck are you saying?"

"Sandro, you sent me two text messages from Alice's phone."

"Now you're really busting my balls. I didn't send you any fucking messages, much less from Alice's phone."

"What is it I don't know?"

"Will you listen to me? I have no idea what you're talking about."

"Tell me!"

Focus. Like when he was at the gym, in that other life, and had to do one last extension with a weight that was too heavy, but he couldn't quit. His energy is drained, only rage remains. And a body now wasted by heroin that has to find the strength to do it. Sandro makes a fist, turns, and punches Enrico in the face. Enrico slams into the wall behind him and stares at Sandro with the look of someone who doesn't understand what's happening. All Sandro can feel is the pain in his hand, his fingers have now started trembling again. Maybe he fractured something.

He caught him smack on the cheekbone. A drop of blood. Enrico takes a tissue and dabs at the wound. Then he looks at him. Sandro feels his eyes on him, as if Enrico were only now seeing him for the first time. He'd like to see in those eyes the same hatred he feels inside, instead it pains him to see something there that resembles pity. He doesn't want his fucking pity. He makes a fist again, but the pain is so intense that this time he moves too slowly and leaves Enrico time to block his arm.

"That's enough, Sandro."

He'd like to answer him, but he's ashamed. For what he has become, for what he just did. For what no one knows. So he breaks free from Enrico's grip and walks away. The cramps of withdrawal become more intense, and he has to lean against a chair to avoid ending up on the floor. A guy eating a sandwich at the bar turns and looks at him with the same expression he'd have if he were looking at a piece of shit he just stepped in. *Come on, Sandro, just a few steps between the chair and the door. Focus. Again. Remember? Strong and handsome like a Greek hero. You can do it.* He leaves the chair and heads off into space. And somehow he manages to make his way out of the bar and into his car.

Enrico goes over to a table and keeps dabbing at his cut. It's still bleeding a little. The place has changed. The tables, with all the inscriptions carved into them, are gone. It's become an Irish pub, sterile and anonymous like all the others.

"It's okay with me if he comes here to pass the time when he's not stoned."

Enrico turns to the voice. A guy he doesn't know, maybe the manager of the place.

"But go settle your problems someplace else. I don't want to see that kind of stuff in here. Got it?"

Too many things to explain. None of which would make sense.

"Don't worry. It won't happen again."

The manager nods: that's the answer he wanted to hear. He goes back to the bar. Exchanges a glance with the guy eating the sandwich.

Enrico leaves.

Outside the pub, the boy is kicking the deflated ball against the wall. When he sees Enrico come out, he catches the ball and stops. He's wearing a red down jacket with an Ironman logo on the chest and a pair of very thick glasses; he has tiny little eyes behind the lenses and a booger sticking out of his nose.

"Do you know Messi?" There's something not right about his voice.

"You like him?" Enrico asks, dabbing at his cheekbone with the bloodstained tissue.

"Messi is the greatest of all."

The boy sniffles. Smiles. Gives the ball a kick and slams it against the wall, continuing his imaginary game.

Sandro drives off, and Enrico's eyes follow the car as it moves away.

It's like a stain that won't come out. The stench of burnt toast that lingers in the kitchen when you forget the bread in the toaster. The ache of a years-old injury that on rainy days starts hurting again. There's nothing you can do, except wait until it passes.

Sandro's car disappears, swallowed up by a time curve. The boy with the Ironman jacket goes on throwing the ball against the wall, without a clear purpose.

His face still hurts, but it's not bleeding anymore. Enrico drops the tissue into a trash bin.

At this point the feeling of no longer belonging to that place is almost liberating. There is nothing left for him here. He'll go back to the house, turn on his laptop, start working on the Remeres project, and Monday morning, after he's signed the papers, he'll leave this place for good.

It's over.

Maybe he had to take that punch. To look Sandro in the eye and say, "That's enough."

Five

Sandro is lying on the bed watching television. The run-in with Enrico made everything more difficult. His anxiety has risen, but he has to wait a little while longer for his fix, otherwise the effect will wear off too soon and the whole weekend schedule will go up in smoke, and then he'll be in danger of doing without for a day.

A day is long and doing without . . . No way . . .

"The second suggestion for the Pizzarotti family is a house two kilometers from San Teodoro, overlooking La Cinta beach." Images scroll by of a house with white walls, a pool, a backyard with thatched umbrellas, and a terrace on a strip of white sand that stretches before a blue sea. "Four bedrooms, kitchen, two living rooms, a den, three baths, and a large terrace on two acres of land. The cost is a little over their budget but . . ."

Click.

"The taipan is the most venomous snake in the world." More images scroll by of the reptile as it slithers among the rocks. It's a strange color, more or less electric blue. Or maybe the plasma screen is completely shot. "It's typically found in Australia and can reach lengths of more than three meters. Its venom is the most toxic and deadly in the world. It is also very fast. Just think—it can reach a speed of sixteen kilometers per hour. It is virtually designed to bite swiftly and with extreme precision. And it is also known for its good memory."

Australia is a shitty place. If something poisonous and deadly exists, you'll find it there for sure. Why would anyone go there? If you want to harm yourself, isn't it simpler to just swallow a bottle of pills? In a moment of weakness, Sandro turns to the bedside table. Maybe he could at least prepare the syringe, that way it'll be ready. But like fuck he'll put it back in the drawer once it's ready.

No, that would be a very bad idea. No way . . .

Click.

"Now Maria Elena is ready to discover her new look." The lanky guy is wearing a suit like that of the Mad Hatter, while the woman with the Targaryen albino hair moves quickly to reveal a mannequin clad in garish colors. The damned plasma screen is definitely off.

Sandro goes on changing channels in the hope of finding something that will grab his attention, so he won't think about the withdrawal cramps that are becoming increasingly intense and unbearable.

Click.

"To make a perfect cheesecake it is very important to work the base well." The fat guy is wearing a white apron, leaning his hands on a work counter where he's arranged bowls, ingredients, spoons, and other rather strange utensils. "We take one hundred and eighty grams of biscuits and crush them. To do so, however, we do not use a food processor, because that would pulverize them, and we'd end up forming a base that's too compact and therefore too hard. Instead we take a napkin, place the biscuits in it, and start kneading them. Like so." His hands work forcefully, crumbling the contents of the napkin. "It's a bit as if this were your brain in here, don't you think?" *Right, that's exactly what it feels like.* "We'll smash it up real good, working the result into an amorphous pap, nice, huh?" *Not really. No, I'd say I don't like what you're doing to my brain, not one little bit.* "So, now that we've prepared the base, let's think about the filling. We take the heroin . . ." *What did that fat guy say?* "We take the heroin powder and dissolve it in a teaspoon of hot water, which we heat with the flame of a gas lighter, not with a cigarette lighter that quickly overheats it, and then add a few drops of lemon juice to facilitate solubility. Finally, to remove any residual solids, we take a metal filter, even a tea strainer your grandmother once used, and pour the preparation through it before filling the insulin syringe with it. Like sooo."

And he finds himself holding the disposable Insumed syringe with the eight-millimeter needle and minimal diameter. Ready to be injected. And so, okay, all defenses surrender. "In the vein it ensures an immediate, intense effect," the pastry chef continues, "while with intramuscular, it's more relaxed, and after a slow start it can take as long as ten minutes to achieve a feeling of well-being." Sandro chooses the second option. The needle penetrates his flesh, the plunger is lowered, and the liquid that works wonders will soon make everything more bearable, including the fat pastry chef who is spreading the cheesecake mixture over the base made from crumbling his brain.

Chiara checks WhatsApp. Margherita hasn't responded to her message. Odd. You can tell she's busy. Saturday night in London is not like Saturday in this lousy place. Maybe she's hanging out with her friends, in a colorful world of aperitifs, cocktails, live music, and fun until dawn.

The history book is on the nightstand, she'll think about that tomorrow. Today is not a good day. It seems things are happening purposely to distract her. And, in an hour, Gibo will come and pick her up to spend the evening together. They'll go for a ride somewhere, sit in the car listening to some music, and he'll talk about something. Then they'll go have a pizza in some place along the Aurelia toward Rome. And after that she hopes he'll take her to the beach. And kiss her. And touch her.

The thought is pleasurable. She lies on the bed, pulls the quilt over herself, and unzips her jeans.

The screen is animated by a tube that changes color and produces a series of hypnotic geometries. Sitting at the table, laptop in front of him, Enrico follows the movements of the screensaver, which switched on some time ago. Under there, somewhere, is his latest attempt to find a solution to the Remeres problem, buried by a tangle of thoughts that went round and round. He follows the lysergic evolutions of the tube and thinks about the inexcusable lack of a command to reset his brain. If Alice had answered that question—*Is there someone else?*—before getting out of the car, it would have all been simpler, but to admit it out loud would be a little like minimizing everything that happened afterward, so he can't do it. That thought must remain as is, unspoken, lost in the bright, colorful trail of a changing tube that glides across a black screen.

The door is locked, the lights are off, the sign on the window with the hours eliminates any doubt: Beta Realty is not open on Saturday afternoons. Maurizio is shut up inside. He said he was going there to check some documents. Just to say something, not worrying too much about whether it sounded true. The computer is turned off. His desk chair is a nearly perfect imitation of a designer piece, a note of class in an office that he retained so he wouldn't have to come in contact with clients. As he sits there, motionless, the smoke from the cigarette he's holding rises in an undisturbed vertical column, geometrically perfect. Maybe Enrico shouldn't have come back. He should have found a way to send him the documents and close the deal by mail. But how could he ever imagine . . .

He can't stop thinking about what Enrico told him. About the messages he received. That phone no longer existed. It had been retrieved and made to disappear. Yet someone used it. And may have found, in that same phone, the messages that Maurizio had written to Alice. So why hadn't that someone ever said anything? Why had he or she remained silent about such a thing? Maybe Alice had deleted them? But then what else could Enrico not know? What else could those words be alluding to? Isn't it obvious? His darling girlfriend and his best friend. A plot so predictable, so trite, like one of those pathetic movies that Betti loads in the DVD player. So then that phone must still exist. And those messages must still be there. All of them.

The light filtering through the small window grows dimmer. Saturday night looms ahead, with the telecast of the nationals qualifying match, Sky TV, the sofa, pizza heated in the oven, and a mug of beer. But it's as if everything has gone flat. Lost its color and definition.

Someone knew about him.

Only Sandro could have that phone. Why has he kept silent?

I punched him. If Sandro were able to think, he would think about that. If the weak electrical impulses filtering through that heroin-cooked brain made sense, that's what they would tell him. *I punched him, my hand hurts, I nearly fell over, right there in the pub. Because he told me that I had sent him some messages. From Alice's phone.*

Alice's phone.

"Sandro." There she is, sitting on the edge of the bed. For his sister, time has not passed.

"Ali . . ."

Sandro nimbly stands up. He feels like he did when he was okay. The muscular, peroxided guy, the Greek hero, is back. He looks at his arms and flexes them, letting the biceps swell under the tight black T-shirt.

"I think you need to explain," his sister says.

He sits down next to her.

"She won't talk to me about it, you know that. I've tried plenty of times," he says, taking her hand. Her skin is so soft. He brings her hand to his face and sniffs the scent that he misses so much. "She knows I'm to blame and she won't say anything, as usual."

"No, you have to tell *him*."

"Enrico?"

"Did you hear what he said? *She* sent him those messages. She wanted to tell him something. Something he doesn't know."

"But then it will all come out. I'll end up in trouble."

"Sandro . . ."

"Ali . . ."

"You're already in trouble." She points to the bed. The scrawny, limp body lying there with a fresh hole in his arm. "It was a mistake to hide everything. Dad thought he was saving you, but he couldn't. You can do it, though. You can tell him. He's looking for the truth. Maybe there's more that's been kept hidden. Maybe if you were to help him find it . . ."

"I'd feel better?"

Alice smiles. She strokes his face. She seems sad. Sandro would never want to see her sad.

"Hey, what's this?" he says, sliding a hand behind her neck, where he knows she's ticklish. Alice laughs. But only for a moment, then she slips away. Sandro hears a sound and turns. Across the room, behind his work counter, the fat pastry chef is still at work. Those huge, tough hands of his are like bricks. They're smeared with mortar. His body looks more and more like that of a gorilla, his face more and more pasty and misshapen.

The light-blue cap.

The Half-Wit stares at him.

"Sandro, will you throw me the ball?"

Six

It's time. Chiara puts on her jacket and zips it up to the chin as usual. The white wires of the earbuds emerge from under the hood. Chris Martin. Cigarettes taken from Maurizio's supply and double-mint chewing gum. She goes down the stairs. Passes the kitchen. Her mother is sitting at the table with the phone to her ear. She looks at her, says something into the phone, and places her hand over it. Chiara removes an earbud.

"Going out?"

"Yep."

"With Gibo?"

"You know that."

"We didn't talk much today, did we?"

"Is there something you have to tell me?"

"Maybe we should talk more."

"Not now, though."

"It wouldn't be polite to keep Mr. Gibo waiting."

"Anything else?"

Betti hesitates.

"Don't be back too late."

Chiara puts the earbud back in and leaves.

Gibo will pick her up at the corner. He doesn't want to stop at her house because he doesn't like the way Betti looks at him. Another thing she wouldn't stand for, if it wasn't Saturday night. There's also the problem of the oil slick and the fact that her street is a dead end.

Her father's car is gone. Strange, usually at this hour they're both already on the couch watching television.

When she gets to the corner, she takes out the cigarettes. She lights one, careful to hide it in the palm of her hand. The sound of a car approaches and soon its headlights. She recognizes Gibo's car, a huge off-road vehicle that feels like a truck when you're inside it. When it stops in front of her, she opens the passenger door, climbs in, and waits for him to give her a kiss like he always does.

"Ciao, Kia," he says.

"Ciao."

"Ciao," a voice from the back seat calls. A girl. She's stretched out, her head leaning against one door and her bare feet propped against the other. She's wearing heavy makeup and the mark of a tattoo shows on her neck.

"My cousin, Rachele," says Gibo.

Chiara doesn't exactly know what to say. But she thinks that maybe for some reason he had to bring her with him. So she smiles at her.

"What time do I have to bring you back?" Gibo asks her.

"At whatever time I want."

Gibo smiles.

"Get it?" Rachele says.

"Of course . . ." says Gibo.

He puts the car in gear, steps on the gas, and zooms off, burning rubber on the asphalt.

"Sweetheart, how come you're home alone? What about your friends?" In Giulia's wonderful world spending Saturday at home, by yourself, is a red flag, a clear sign that something is wrong.

"I had some work to do."

"Remeres?"

"Right."

"It must be really fascinating to compel you to spend Saturday night on it."

"And how's the party?"

"A nightmare, I swear. The caterers arrived half an hour late. I mean, *half an hour*. Virginia and the Evil Sisters, instead, arrived half an hour early, of course, because otherwise they wouldn't have found a taxi. So while the caterers were still preparing the canapés, the bitches started roaming around the house and posting pictures on Facebook. Now, it's just as well we're moving, because our house is all over their profiles. And then, as the others were arriving, the caterers were still arranging the *vol-au-vent* on the trays."

"A tragedy."

"The tragedy is that you're not here, my love."

He can just picture her. In the midst of all her "friends"—a term that, with the help of Facebook (which Giulia is virtually addicted to), has excessively expanded her semantic field, filling their apartment with her girlfriends from the gym, her aperitif friends, her friends from the boutique, friends from the shiatsu center, and even friends from a Facebook book club, which Giulia joined pretending to be a passionate reader while actually just wanting to find a book to surprise Enrico with, instead of the usual sweater gift. And he imagines her there, beautiful and glowing, wearing an evening dress, dispensing kisses and smiles while glued to her phone. After she gets off the phone with him, she'll call her mother and after that her sister. Yet, for Enrico, at this moment there is only the tube that continues gliding through a confined space. It's like a question that keeps looking for an answer but can't find it. Because there's no way out. The tube can't get out of the screen. So the fact that it appears to be looking for a way out is only an optical illusion.

Giulia talks a while longer, then abruptly has to go because someone she must greet has just arrived.

And the silence returns.

Enrico looks down at the laptop's keyboard and finds his old phone on it. When did he put it there? He reads the display and the same message is still there.

I thought you wanted to know, and instead you chose to forget.

It's bone-crushingly cold tonight, McClane. Enzo Porretta puts on his uniform and zips up the jacket with the security agency's logo sewn on it. *On the job, Lieutenant.* He studies himself in the mirror, assuming a tough guy look. In this light, with that peach fuzz on his face that won't grow but seems heavier tonight, that expression in the eyes that look like two dark slits, he and Bruce Willis have something in common. And, with the cap pulled down, you can't even see the balding.

"On the job," he says to his reflection.

Regulation belt. Instead of a gun, he still only has a flashlight, but the agency's manager promised him that he will soon be supplied with a weapon as well. They just need to settle a few things regarding the permits and then they'll give him a gun.

He goes downstairs, opens the door, and steps out. It gets dark early and by this hour the streetlights are all lit. Of course, if there were a big street around here with a hot dog stand and a steaming manhole, it would be a different story, instead of this lousy little town where the only place a group of East German terrorists, like the one led by Hans Gruber in *Die Hard*, could take people hostage is the parish hall where the senior volunteers' dinner is held on Saturday night.

Shit.

He gets in the company car, arranges all his things, and heads for the Fuorimano, where Saverio is preparing a nice takeout with hot dog and fries, which he will eat in the car like his colleagues in New York do.

◆ ◆ ◆

"You're Margherita's sister, right?" Rachele says from the back seat.

"Yeah, you know her?

"My brother knew her. They went to high school together."

"Do I know him?"

"Francesco Dallei."

"Don't know him."

"He says Margherita had some problem."

"A big problem, loser friends."

"A mental problem, like a breakdown."

Chiara turns to face the back seat.

"My sister didn't have any fucking breakdown. You can tell that to your brother."

"Okay, okay, what the fuck? Take it easy."

"This is a shitty town, baby," Gibo says. "They're quick to spread rumors. People don't have jack shit to do and they'd rather talk about other people's shit. But, tonight, we're here to relax, right?"

"Riiiiight," says Rachele, stretching herself as far as the car's interior will allow.

"Hey, girl, everything okay?" Gibo asks.

Chiara is still looking out the window, at the houses gliding by, the glow of lights, the wet, deserted road. The fact is she doesn't like to hear that kind of crap about her sister. What's insane is that her mother sees it exactly as Gibo does, maybe it takes her much longer to say the same thing, but in the end that's the gist of it: people mind other people's business. The truth is that Margherita may have had her problems, but who doesn't have problems in a shithole like this? One thing is for sure, she was right to leave. The other sure thing is that sooner or later Chiara will join her. And that's a happy thought, the kind that could make you fly like Peter Pan. She turns to Gibo, smiles, crinkles her eyes, and nods.

"All good."

◆　◆　◆

It's as if everything were coming in waves. Sandro is lying on the bed, floating on heroin. He would like to do what Alice told him, get off the bed and go to Enrico's to tell him the thing about the phone. After talking with her, it's as if doing this has become the center of his universe. But then everything is engulfed by something else, a sensation of calmness, serenity, which is so sweet to sink into. Then the wave recedes and that thing he has to do comes back. Now the voices are gone. He's alone. If he could really talk to Enrico, maybe he would stop seeing the Half-Wit every time he shoots up. "Sandro, will you throw me the ball?" He tries moving a foot. His feet still hurt. *Maybe I'll wait till tomorrow,* he thinks. *But maybe tomorrow I won't remember it. And he said he was leaving. And then how will I find him?*

The foot moves. But it's still too heavy. How come this bed doesn't crash to the floor with a weight like this on it? He has to move like the taipan snake, which has a good memory, is very swift, and is the most venomous in the world. He feels it slithering inside him. Three meters of power and speed. Three meters of creeping death. Sandro grinds his teeth, hisses, contracts his muscles, and after a period of time, which expands and then shrinks senselessly, like a Jim Morrison walk in the desert with a shaman, he sits up on the bed. But he feels the wave coming again, here it is. Calmness, serenity. This sweet lethargy that envelops you and lets you rest your head, like this . . . Lie back . . . Relax . . .

"Fuck." He opens his eyes again. "Come on, Sandro, get up. You're over it. I can feel you're getting over it."

The taipan snake's strike leaves the enemy no way out.

He's not sure how, but he finds himself on his feet.

◆ ◆ ◆

Gibo stops the car right in front of the sea. They're practically on the beach, that four by four isn't afraid of anything.

"Shall we toke up?" he says.

"About time," Rachele replies, though she had seemed to be asleep.

"For what?" Chiara asks.

"For some *maria*," Gibo says, opening the glove compartment. He takes out a bag with a bulging packet of grass and the usual Smoking Brown longs that he has learned to roll with one hand even while driving.

"Let's move to the back, come on. We'll be more comfortable."

Without getting out of the car, they squeeze between the front seats and climb in back with Rachele. Gibo, in the middle, prepares the joint. It's ready in a second and Gibo lights up. He blows on the tip to get rid of the residual cigarette paper that flutters away, then takes a deep drag, holding the smoke in his lungs as he passes it to Chiara.

She likes marijuana. It tastes good and makes her happy. It's not like that synthetic crap that turns your brain to mush and you never recover.

Gibo looks for some suitable music on the iPod connected to the car stereo system and puts on a Pink Floyd album. According to him, as he's already had occasion to explain, they wrote their songs while they were stoned, so you can only understand certain things if you get in tune with those frequencies.

"What's it called?" Chiara asks him.

"The album?"

"Yeah."

"*The Dark Side of the Moon.*"

"Not bad."

"Not bad at all."

They go on passing the joint until Gibo takes a last drag and tosses what's left of the butt, smoked down to the filter, out the window.

Chiara leans back against the seat and loosens up.

Rachele, however, unzips Gibo's pants.

"What the fuck is your cousin doing?" Chiara asks.

"She's not really my cousin . . ."

"Yeah, but . . ."

"Let's have some fun, come on," Gibo says. "You two go down on me together and I'll film it. Then we'll watch it and smoke another joint."

Chiara hasn't yet figured out what's happening when Rachele already has Gibo's cock in her mouth. Rachele looks at the phone in his hand, filming her, then pulls away and smiles.

"Come on," she says to Chiara.

"No way."

"Come on, Chiara," Gibo says, his smile slack from the weed.

"We're just having a little fun," Rachele says.

"Have fun then."

Chiara opens the door and gets out.

"Hey, where are you going? Come back here," Gibo says.

"Go to hell. You and your cousin."

She slams the door behind her and walks away. Her head is spinning a bit, but she knows the way back to town.

She zips up her jacket and pulls up the hood, but no Chris for now, later maybe. Right now she's really steamed, and she doesn't want to ruin those songs forever.

The coast road is in total darkness.

Gibo is just a sad little dickhead. She still has to decide if what galls her the most is the fact that she had him all wrong or that Betti had clearly seen through him before she did.

She looks around.

It's pitch black.

Seven

The wave arrives at the wrong moment. At the curve, he's on the verge of losing it. Sandro manages to look up an instant before the car is about to take the plunge. He'd taken the curve straight, and would have crashed into the trees otherwise.

"Come on, Sandro!" he yells to wake himself up.

He puts the car into reverse and backs up onto the road. His eyes, wide with fear, suddenly close. He can't get over the narrow escape he's just had, his blood is racing at breakneck speed, his heart is pounding in his head like a hammer. He drives off again, begins the descent. He leans against the steering wheel and feels a trickle of drool dribbling down. Here comes the wave. How beautiful. It's all calm. Feel how the car glides down the hill. How it floats, how it flies. *I just need to lean here for a second and . . .*

"Shit!" He comes to abruptly and grabs the wheel. The road. Everything is okay.

He reaches the bottom of the hill and turns onto the provincial road.

And after fifty meters a carabiniere appears with a raised stop sign.

◆ ◆ ◆

Not only is it so dark that if you're not careful you could end up in a ditch, but it's also freezing cold tonight. Chiara has let her anger simmer down and plugged in her earbuds, so Chris can keep her company on this walk she wasn't planning on.

She took the route past the old bridge, and left the coast road behind. In a few minutes, she'll be back in town. What a shitty evening. And she doesn't feel much like going home. For one thing, the pot is still swirling around in her head and she's not yet up to facing her mother, who will be anxious for an explanation as to why she's back so early.

She brings up WhatsApp.

Vale . . . what are you doing?

She crosses the bridge.

Kia!!! I'm at Fede's . . .

Alone?

Yep ;) what's up?

Nothing, a shitty night, I'll tell you tomorrow.

Wanna come here?

No, thanks anyway.

Vale is with her boyfriend, Chiara doesn't feel like butting in. Maybe there'll be someone at the station bar. But she doesn't want to seem desperate. The best thing is to stop here, at the first available low wall, and listen to Chris and *A Rush of Blood to the Head* with a few cigarettes—fortunately tonight, at least, she has some.

Walking past the first houses in town, she observes the lights through the windows. They have that yellowish color. She takes out an earbud to listen. In each house a TV is on. The clatter of dishes, someone shouting. There must be a soccer game. Of course, Italy's match against that team from the East where all the caregivers are usually from. She hears the voices of the sportscasters, who know the names of all the players by heart and recognize them right away, even the foreign ones. Because soccer players are the only foreigners people like. Maybe because they're filthy rich. Someone swears loudly, it must have been a penalty kick. There's really something wrong with some people's lives if they get so excited about things like that. She sits on the steps of a doorway. Puts the earbud back in. She lights a cigarette and lets the opening of "Politik" explode in her ears. And, just then, she sees her father's car turn the corner.

It's okay, Sandro. Everything's fine. No problem. So they'll put you inside. What can you do? You'll have a little peace and quiet, put an end to all this crap, and that's it. In fact, you know what I'll do? I'll tell him right now, as soon as I roll down the window and the cop points the light at me. I'll tell him. Look, I'll say, I'm hyped up on heroin. There's not much to add. My life got mired in deep shit many years ago.

"You have a headlight out. Did you know that?" the carabiniere says.

"What?"

"Your left headlight, it's out."

"My left headlight."

"Right."

"Yeah, in fact it just blew out."

"You should take care of it."

"I'll take care of it tomorrow, first thing."

"Tomorrow is Sunday."

"That's true, let's say Monday and let it go at that."

"Everything okay?"

"Hunky-dory."

"Get it fixed, these roads are dark."

"Sure thing."

"On your way now."

"Night."

What the hell, Sandro, if only you'd had a stroke of luck like that when you really needed it. Fuck. I came through just fine this time. He takes a breath. Never had anything like that happened, didn't even ask for his license. *How the hell did you manage not to puke all over him, the shape you're in? Because it's a sign, that's why. Fuck. Because it's no accident that Alice said those things, it's no accident that I managed to stand up in this condition. No. It's no accident that the cop didn't notice anything and only told me about the headlight. It means that what I'm doing makes sense. Fuck, maybe it's the first time in all these shitty years of crap that what I'm doing really makes sense. Holy fucking shit. I'll go to Enrico's and tell him the thing about the phone, that way maybe he'll be able to talk about it, with her. That's what I should have done. That's why I'm here. That's why I didn't die all these years. It's because of this night. This thing I have to do. Right, little sister?*

"Sure, that's right."

"And then I'll feel better?"

Chiara hides behind a hedge. She lets the car go by. It's him, she recognizes him. But what is he doing here? Where is he going? Why isn't he at home in front of the television? He should be watching the game too, with his anchovy pizza. The car turns the corner, Chiara follows it and hides behind the side of the building. The car stops, but the engine remains running. She sees someone coming from across the street. It's that Mazzei, from the beauty salon. She has that damn dog of hers on a leash, the little turd acting as if he were possessed by an Egyptian demon. The woman approaches her father's car.

She stops. Ties the dog's leash to a pole with a "No Entry" sign on it. He opens the car door and she gets in.

They embrace.

They make out like a couple of teenagers. Clinging to one another, they still manage to catch their breath and talk.

Chiara takes out her earbuds. It would really be a shame if Chris were to witness such a sleazy scene like that. How sordid. Mazzei.

He says something to her. She nods. They smile. Then they kiss again. This goes on for about ten minutes. When she gets out of the car and unties her dog, "The Scientist" is playing on the iPhone. Chiara is surprised to realize that her father and the beautician were necking throughout the duration of "In My Place" and "God Put a Smile Upon Your Face." And as she watches the car move away, hidden behind the building, she feels such a sense of disgust rise inside her that what Gibo and that bitch Rachele left her with seems like nothing in comparison.

"Hey, what are you doing there?"

Chiara turns and sees a guy up at a window, lighting a cigarette. He's on the other side of the building, so he didn't see her father's car drive away.

"Talking to me?"

"Who else, girlie?"

"Minding my own business, why?"

"And I'm calling the cops, bitch."

The guy goes inside. Great. That's all she needs. Because then maybe they'll catch her with her pupils still dilated and undoubtedly figure out that she smoked a joint. The station bar isn't far. She pulls up her hood and crosses the street. Next to the pole with the "No Entry" sign, Mazzei's disgusting dog left a ringlet of pungent shit.

A group of guys speaking a strange Eastern European language is sitting in a corner of the bar watching the game on television when she enters. There are espresso cups on the table and a bottle that looks like grappa. Their faces are red. Maybe because it's so hot in here, or maybe because of the alcohol. Chiara finds a table away from them. All she wants to do is cry, but she can't. Not now.

She takes out her iPhone. Opens the text app.

Everything is fucked up, I want to stay with you. Come and get me?

And she sends it to her grandmother.

Okay, now it's easy. Come on, Sandro. Remember to leave it in reverse because the hand brake doesn't hold. Just open the door, take a breath, wait for the wave to pass, and cross the street. Remember to put it in reverse. Then turn on the indicator signal. Remember the hand brake. There, that's it. One big thrust, like the taipan snake's strike. Swift and deadly. And we're on our feet. A deep breath, that's it. See, it's not hard. A step. That's right. Where the hell did Enrico's house go? Oh, there it is. I missed it. You get distracted for one minute and they move everything around here. Another step. Thaaaat's it. Doing great, Sandro, come on, otherwise we'll get to that gate by tomorrow morning. And what if he isn't home? Shit, that would be a problem. I should have called first. But the number, where the hell would I have found it?

"In the phone directory, right?"

"Dad, what are you doing here?"

Giancarlo is there, in front of him. He's holding the hunting rifle.

"What do you think you're going to solve?"

"I . . . I think I want to do it," Sandro replies.

"You *think* you want to do it? That's always been your problem, *you think*. If you'd ever been sure of anything in your life, you wouldn't have ended up like this."

"I'm sorry, but all those nightmares . . . I . . . I couldn't shake them."

"And he'll help you do that?"

Lift your head up. It's just bullshit, Sandro. Open your eyes, you were falling asleep again, weren't you? Hang in there, one more step. Come on, we can do it. That's what we came here for, don't you see, Dad? We came here for a specific reason.

But I think I forgot to put it in reverse.

Fuck, I'm sure I forgot.

I'll just stop here a minute. I'll take a little breather, and then I'd better go and put it in reverse, otherwise the car will take off on me.

There, I'll just rest a second.

See how calm everything is, quiet, nothing is moving. Feel how peaceful it is . . .

The Supremo Hot Dog: half a baguette with half a pound of hot sausage sprinkled with cheese and sauerkraut, along with spicy home fries. Mayonnaise everywhere, even on his uniform. A greasy streak right on the chest. *What the fuck, Lieutenant McClane.* The sandwich is just what he needed, though, on this cold, lonely night.

A call.

"Porretta."

"Did you go by Via delle Ortiche?"

"I'm going, Central."

"Make sure you drive by a couple of times tonight. They left me a note."

"Roger."

"Here we go again. Who the hell is Roger?"

"The usual, Central. It means I understood."

"So then tell me you understood, Enzo, please. Already I'm pissed off because I have to watch the game here on this crappy TV that makes all the players look deformed. If you're going to make it worse with your crackpot ideas, I'll never get through it."

"Enjoy the game, Central. I'll see to things out here."

"Go to hell."

The Supremo is half gone. McClane sets it on the seat and puts the car in gear. The agency vehicle glides into the night, headed for Via delle Ortiche. Who knows what the genius who called it that was thinking. Why not number the streets, like they do in New York? It would be so much simpler than having to come up with all these idiotic names. It might make sense to name the street after a person, maybe someone who was an important figure, who did something, like Clint Eastwood, but to name it Nettles, after the dumbest plant that exists, is really stupid. At that rate, there should be a Via della Zanzara, for the mosquito. Via della Merda, for the shit you step in. He takes another bite of the Supremo.

By the time he turns onto Via delle Ortiche, a street with a slight downhill slope, there are two mayonnaise streaks on his uniform. They run parallel on his chest, like two medals of valor.

Here, though, there's something wrong.

He plunges his hand into the bag of spicy home fries and stuffs a few in his mouth. He chews slowly.

"Oh sweet Jesus."

He pulls the car over and climbs out.

In the middle of the street there is a man. Lying on the ground.

"Oh fucking shit."

"Bettina."

"Mama?"

"I spoke with Chiara."

"What? You know that . . ."

"She came to me. She sent me a text."

"And who gave her the number? Tell me."

"Your daughter is a mess, she needs me."

"No one here needs you, Mama."

"Can *you* handle the situation?"

"There is no situation to handle."

"Betti, honey, I just want to help. We have a family to think about."

Silence.

"Mama . . ."

"I'll bring her home."

Enrico quit watching the tubes. He made himself a sandwich with tuna and olives, took off his shoes, poured a beer into a glass, and stretched out on the couch to watch the game. A sound. Insistent.

Enrico looks around. What was that?

Again.

The intercom.

Who can it be?

He gets up to find out. Only now does he realize that there's a new intercom. It has video.

He's not sure how it works, but after intuitively pressing some keys he manages to turn it on. In the monitor is a guy he doesn't know. He looks like a traffic cop or maybe a security guard. Maybe he's the one the agency sent.

"Yes?" he says.

"Good evening, I'm Porretta, from the security agency. There's a problem here."

"Excuse me, what did you say?"

"Yeah, there's a guy, he's on the ground, he's injured and keeps repeating your name."

"Whose name?"

"Yours, that is, the one that's written outside here, I mean . . . Sarti. He keeps saying that he has to talk to Enrico Sarti."

"But who is he? What is he saying?"

"Look, I know it seems odd, if you ask me I would advise you not to open the door because the thing reeks of a scam, if you know what I mean. But there really is a car out here, a black sedan, a Ford Focus I'd guess, that crashed into a tree, one of those out front here, maybe a pine, I'd say a big pine tree, you know the one? And in the middle of the street there's this guy. His name is Bastiani. He's pretty much a junkie and was already cruising around here the other night. Maybe I could explain things to you, except this guy is hurt and I have to call one-one-eight, actually I think I should already have done that, in terms of protocol, I mean, emergency procedure, or maybe I should call the carabinieri first, right now I can't remember exactly . . . What do you think? Can you hear me? Mr. Sarti, are you still there?"

Eight

Maurizio opens the window in the office to let out the smoke. He doesn't even know how long he's been there. He checks the time. Too long. There was a game tonight. He retreated here to think, but he hasn't come up with anything. Someone, most likely Sandro, knows about him and Alice. What does that mean? Really hard to say. Still, the girl was murdered and he didn't tell anyone about their relationship. Difficult to know what might happen if it were to come out now, but it certainly wouldn't sound good. And the other night, on the news, there was that story about a murder case that was reopened nearly twenty years later. Simona, he needs her. He picks up the phone and sends her a text.

Can you come down for ten minutes?

He puts the phone on the table and stares at it. But if he keeps staring at it, nothing will ever come to him, that's for sure. So he turns and goes to the bathroom. He pees with the door open behind him, a dark, blurred silhouette against the yellowish glow of the light. The phone's display on the table is bright, and before he comes back the little balloon appears.

I'll take Dudy out. I'll be down in fifteen minutes.

The place where they meet when they need to see each other, even for a few minutes, even just to say good night, is always the same. It's a secluded spot. Just turn a corner and there are only a few windows, but they are always closed at that hour. Besides, he can't very well send her walking on the coast road like a hooker. They're also friends and people know it, so what's the harm if he, passing by, sees her and they stop to say hello?

Maurizio drives slowly. Unhurriedly. The first houses in town appear, it's a quiet area. Farther on is the station bar, but you can't see it from here. It's only a back road that continues on to the bridge that leads to the coast road.

He stops and the engine automatically shuts down. He checks around to see if there's anyone at the windows. All closed.

Simona comes along with Dudy on a leash. She's wearing a light coat and little else, he knows, under it. Black stockings for sure, and a miniskirt short enough to reveal the part of her tanned thigh that arouses him uncontrollably. She's a fantastic woman. Thirty-seven years old and a body that cries out for sex with each breath. Her husband is at least thirty years older and is a bit winded, but his bank account adequately makes up for it: he bought her the beauty salon and provides her the life she dreamed of.

When she gets to the car, she smiles in that way that changes the course of Maurizio's blood, concentrating it in one part of his body.

She ties Dudy's leash to the pole, because ever since the time he bit Maurizio's ankle, he has to wait outside.

She climbs in and they kiss. They cling to one another. They kiss again.

"Ciao, little mouse," Simona says.

"Ciao, little mouse."

"I miss you so much, you know?"

"I miss you too . . ."

"What are you doing tonight?"

"I have a little work," he says.

"You're always working, poor baby."

"How about we take a vacation?"

"Where would we go?"

"To a spa, we'll enjoy three days of massages, hot stones, mud baths, and unbridled sex."

"Do you mean it?"

"Sooner or later you'll take a refresher course, right?"

"When?" she asks.

"Next week."

"My little mouse, how I love you!"

They kiss again. They cling even tighter. She opens the coat: she's wearing the stockings. Maurizio slips a hand between her thighs.

"If you do that, you know I won't be able to stop," Simona whispers in his ear.

"Then don't stop."

"Not here, little mouse." She closes up the raincoat.

"You do that to me on purpose, don't you?"

"I like to keep you revved up, you know."

"See you tomorrow?"

"Monday, two o'clock, come and have a nude sunbath."

Simona opens the door and gets out of the car. She kisses her fingertips—her nails are polished red—and blows the kiss to Maurizio. She unties Dudy and realizes that he has left a pile of poo. She rummages in her pocket, looking for a plastic bag, but she didn't take any before coming down. Never mind, it's very small. She walks off, swaying on her heels.

Maurizio starts back toward home. When he gets to the corner, however, he sees a car go by. It's Sandro's Focus and it's heading toward Via delle Ortiche.

It's an instant, just enough time to clear away Simona's scent and be struck by a not quite fully formed thought. Without even realizing that he's made a decision that is surely wrong for so many reasons, he follows the car.

The black Focus stops about twenty meters before Enrico's gate, in the middle of the street. Maurizio approaches at a safe distance, but after killing the engine, he remains inside, watching. Sandro emerges from his car, staggering. He's definitely wasted. And not just a little either. He looks around and seems to be looking for something. He takes a step, then another, and stops. He seems to be talking to someone, but there isn't another living soul around. His head drops to his chest. He'll fall to the ground at any moment. He recovers and takes another step, then another and another, almost all the way across the street, heading toward Enrico's gate. Before he reaches the other side, however, he stops again. His head drops as before. He looks back, toward the car. He puts a hand to his forehead, as if trying to remember something, but his legs give way. He falls to the ground.

Is he the one who has Alice's phone? And could he have it with him now?

Maurizio looks around. There's nobody. He gets out of the car. He walks down the street trying to stay in the shadows, keeping to the edge of the wooded area on the right. He approaches Sandro. He seems to be asleep. More than asleep—in a coma.

Just the right time to look for that damn phone. And, if anyone were to see him there, bent over that junkie lying in the street, he can always say he was trying to help him.

He rummages through his pockets, but doesn't find anything. Only a packet of cigarettes with a slim lighter tucked inside.

Shit.

He walks over to Sandro's car. It's unlocked. He climbs in, then ducks down and starts searching.

"Where did you put it, you shitty crackhead? Where do you keep it?"

It's not in here. Maybe it's in the back, in one of the door compartments. He gets out and slides into the back seat. He keeps looking, under the floor mats, in the pockets. Nothing. He straightens up and realizes that Sandro has gotten up. He's standing in the street, looking toward the car.

Maurizio ducks down.

Shit again. If he comes over to the car, what the fuck will he tell him?

But while he's crouching there, he hears something release and the car starts rolling. What's happening? Out of the corner of his eye he sees that the hand brake is either not set or is not pulled up all the way. He reaches for the lever, but it's stuck.

The street slopes downhill.

The car picks up speed.

He grabs the lever with two hands, pulls up as hard as he can, but the bastard won't budge.

He tries stretching toward the pedals to press the foot brake with one hand, but they are too far away and he can't fit through the two front seats.

Then comes the thump.

He just has time to straighten up and see, through the rearview mirror, that Sandro is on the ground again. Meanwhile the car has swerved off the road and is about to hit a tree head-on.

Maurizio bangs his head against the window. For a moment he feels as if he is going to lose consciousness, but then he comes to. He's injured, however. Bleeding. He's messed things up but good.

He crawls out of Sandro's car. Goes over to the body lying on the ground. He hears him mumbling something.

"I don't have the ball . . . Go away . . . Shitty hand brake . . ."

He's still alive.

Call for help? And tell them what? That story about the phone? Say he wanted to rob the junkie and ran him over by mistake? Yeah sure, you know how long a fucked-up story like that will hold up? You know how many things will come out, one after the other? Too many. Good-bye Simona and good-bye spa and good-bye unbridled sex, which he could use badly right now. And then there's everything else to think about. He can't wreck it all now. And that phone isn't even here. Is there a way to squirm out of this mess? Yes. Maurizio knows how. And he knows there's only one way.

He runs to his car. Gets in. Looks around. Waits a few more seconds, but there's nothing moving. Around here, at this time of year, there's no one. The houses are all vacant. This he knows for sure: he's the one who leases them.

The sound of his phone makes him jump. It's Betti. The face in the photo recorded in his contacts belongs to a distant world, in which his wife was still able to smile at him. A drop of blood falls on the display. Maurizio takes the window-wiping cloth from the side pocket of the car door and dabs the blood on his head. He starts the car, puts it in gear, and drives away.

"What's up?"

"There's a problem with Chiara."

"What's the problem?"

"I don't know, but my mother is going to look for her."

Nine

The flashing yellow indicator lights up and the electronic gate begins to slide open. Enzo takes a step back and waits for the homeowner. Sarti, with whom he talked on the video intercom, arrives out of breath, his shoes unlaced, his shirt untucked, and his jacket thrown on hastily.

"Good evening," he says as soon as he steps through the gate, with that overly polite manner that those who have houses around here rub your nose in.

"Evening," Enzo says. "I was passing by on my security rounds and found him like that."

He points to the guy's body lying in the middle of the street. He looks like a squashed bug, half dead, all scrunched up but still moving. Sarti runs over to him and stoops down.

"He's the guy I caught the other night, right here. He was spying on you," Enzo explains.

"I know him."

"Look, I'll call Central headquarters," Enzo says. "I have a phone in the car."

He walks over to the agency car. As he's retrieving the cell phone, he watches the two men in the middle of the street, illuminated by his car's headlights. It looks like the guy on the ground is talking. Maybe he's still talking crap. Some junkies should just stay in a rehab center and not go around being a pain in the ass.

"Central, someone's been injured," he says as soon as they answer.

"Porretta, what are you talking about? Who's injured?"

"He answers to the name of Alessandro Bastiani. Or rather, at the moment he isn't really answering, but anyhow, that's his name, confirmed by a witness."

"What the hell are you saying?"

"An accident, Central, at least that's the most likely assumption right now, but we need the paramedics."

As he spells out the street name and house number, the guy who came out of the house, Sarti, motions him over. Enzo hikes up his pants, grabbing his belt with the flashlight and everything else, pulls the cap lower on his head, and goes up to the witness.

"What is it?" he says as soon as he joins him.

"Listen to me closely." From Sarti's first words he can tell that this story is not yet over, not by a long shot. "I have to leave. I have to do something very important. When the police arrive, tell them I'll be back as soon as possible. Take care of this man and then let me know how he is."

"But did the injured guy tell you anything?"

"I know him. He's a friend of mine."

"Yeah, but did he say what happened? Because he didn't seem very lucid, he was speaking weirdly."

"He told me something important, which is why I have to go now."

"I don't know if you should leave now, you're kind of a witness . . ."

"I didn't see anything. What I have to say I can tell them later. The house is open. If you need anything, go on in."

So okay, it was a shitty night anyway, he'd already had a feeling. *A burning sensation, Lieutenant McClane.* And so he sits on the pavement next to the injured man and crosses his legs.

"How do you feel?" he asks him, enunciating the words clearly, so maybe the junkie will understand.

"I could use another one," Bastiani says. His voice is barely a whisper, but he sounds more coherent.

"You need something?"

"It's coming. I just have to wait."

"What's coming?"

"The wave."

"The wave?"

"Yeah, now I can even sleep."

"If you hit your head, generally speaking you should try to stay awake."

"Here it comes."

Enzo looks around: What wave is this guy talking about?

"You see a wave? You think you're at the beach?"

"It's just a little slower."

The guy is out of his head. Who knows what he's talking about. He must have hit the pavement hard when he fell. Better to play along with him. Enzo tightens his lips in an understanding expression and nods.

"No problem, we'll stay here on the beach and catch some sun, nice and quiet, no wave will get us, you'll see."

The crackhead is delirious, and the most absurd thing is that the other guy, Sarti, took off like a rocket because of something that this one here told him. A bunch of lunatics. The one small hope of redeeming the situation is if Ekaterina is on duty at the Misericordia. If so, maybe she'll come and see that he's saving someone. And these mayonnaise smears on his uniform might look like bloodstains, like the ones that are always found on McClane. Ekaterina has such a beautiful name, because she comes from someplace in Russia. Everyone butchers it into Cate, Cati, Caterina. But you can tell it pleases her when he calls her by her real name, because she always smiles at him in return.

The cokehead, however, mustn't fall asleep.

"Stay awake, come on. Try to tell me your name."

"Me . . . ?"

"Yes, you, of course . . . Can you tell me your name?"

"I am the taipan snake."

Enrico recognizes the profile of the farmhouse as he approaches, driving along the last stretch of the provincial road to Carrubo. A nocturnal, spectral vision. Jacques Spitz's aging present from *The Eye of Purgatory*. It is both the same as he remembered and unrecognizable in its deterioration. Peeling shutters on the windows, overgrown grass, climbing ivy that has swallowed up much of the building. The unfinished expansion that looks like a ruin. It looks like something that was, and instead it is something that has never been.

The only sound is that of the car door slamming behind him as he walks to the door. He has his old phone in his pocket. Those messages. He knows now who sent them. He knows now that an answer awaits him in there.

He follows Sandro's instructions. The few words he'd managed to tell him as he struggled through the nightmares that plagued him, that were taking him farther and farther away.

The door is unlocked. Enrico goes in. Inside it is dark and silent.

There is a staircase leading upstairs. Before going up, though, he must first go to the kitchen. He must do everything as Sandro explained it to him.

He opens the fridge, takes out a carton of milk, and fills a glass. The cookie tin is beside the sink. They are dry biscuits, each shaped like a different animal. There are kittens, teddy bears, and elephants. He takes a handful, making sure that there is at least one of each kind, and puts them on a plate.

He leaves the kitchen and goes up the stairs. No need to look for a light switch: the shutters are open and the night is luminous.

Step by step, a sound begins to penetrate the silence. At first it's far away, remote. Little more than a distant crackle. Then it materializes. A voice, then some cheerful music, one of those South American tunes that people dance to, moving as a group.

He reaches the top of the stairs and starts down the corridor. From under the last door, at the end of the hall, comes a faint bluish glow.

He knocks. No answer. It's only an attempt, it won't be easy and he won't necessarily succeed. But he has to try.

He opens the door.

Luciana Bastiani, Giancarlo's wife, the mother of Sandro and Alice, is sitting in a big armchair beside the bed. She's wearing a flowered robe and a pair of padded slippers. Her white hair falls almost to the floor. Next to the door, on a chest of drawers, a big TV set is turned on to that program with the famous people who dance.

"Good evening, Luciana," Enrico says. "Sandro had a problem. I've brought your dinner."

No reply.

Enrico enters and approaches her. The woman's gaze is fixed on the TV. Not a move. Even back then she suffered from nerves and alcohol problems, now not much of her seems to be left, apart from the little that a desperate drug addict has been able to keep alive.

"I'll put your milk and cookies on the nightstand."

He carefully arranges the glass and saucer among the pill bottles, used tissues, and a big hairbrush. He tries to find enough space without moving anything.

When he turns around, she's staring at him.

The impact of those eyes, of that gaze on him, is unexpected. Enrico wanted a reaction, and now that he has managed to prompt one, he is almost frightened.

"Luciana, I'm Enrico. Remember?"

She goes on staring at him, not saying a word.

"Sandro had a problem, but don't worry, later they'll let us know how he is."

Nothing.

"An accident, in front of my house."

Those eyes planted on him are making him uncomfortable.

"He'd come to tell me something. It's not easy to talk about it now. But see, as a result of a series of circumstances, I found some messages on my phone. Here, wait. I have it in my pocket. Right here. There, you see, this was my old phone, the one I had at the time I was going out with your daughter. With Alice. I had left it at my house, on Via delle Ortiche, turned on. It was plugged in and must have remained on for several days before they took it away with the rest of my stuff, so they could rent the house. See, the fact is that during those days, after the funeral, a number of messages arrived. And two of them came from Alice's number. Here, you see, these two."

But she doesn't look at the phone, she just keeps staring at him.

"Here, there's this one. I'll read it to you: 'I thought you wanted to know, and instead you chose to forget.' I . . . I assure you that it isn't so."

Those eyes on him.

"Sandro told me something," he continues, trying to get through to her. "I went to look for him today. Because after seeing these messages, I was convinced that he had Alice's phone. I was sure he had kept it with him. So I went looking for him and he told me that Alice had left her phone at home that night, because she made a mistake and went out with another phone, the one you all used for the restaurant."

Luciana continues to stare at him, expressionless.

"I never wanted to forget. And if I had known that there were things I didn't know, I would have done anything to find out what they were."

The distance contracts. Time falls back and, superimposing itself, is erased. Enrico had never felt so close to that night. Emotion hits him.

He feels his stomach tighten, his breathing becomes shallow, his eyes sting and well up. Tears.

"Sandro told me that you had it, that telephone. That you kept your daughter's phone with you. Sandro told me that you watched over it constantly so he let you keep it."

Enrico is crying. He's searching for something in those eyes that are boring into him. But it's as if they were letting him drown, indifferent. Trying to get a firm grip on himself, he goes to the window and looks out. The air in the room is heavy. It smells of sweat and medicine. What had he thought he would find?

"You must wonder why I didn't say anything."

The voice comes from behind him. Enrico turns. Luciana's expression has changed. There's life there now.

"About what?"

Luciana looks at him and seems to see him for the first time.

"Enrico . . ." she says.

"What didn't you say anything about?" he urges her.

"The reporters wrote a lot of things about her. I didn't want them to write that too," she says, reaching out to the bedside table to take the glass of milk. Enrico helps her, bringing it to her. "She wasn't like the way they described her. You know that. You're a good boy, you knew her well." She takes a sip of milk and hands the glass to Enrico, who puts it back. She wipes her lips on the sleeve of her robe. "Enrico . . . I waited so long for you."

"I'm sorry. I was . . . I . . ."

"I know, we all were."

"Was it you, Luciana, who sent me those messages?"

"I thought you would answer."

"I assure you I would have, but when you saw that I didn't answer, couldn't you have found me some other way?"

Luciana looks at him, smiling. She raises a hand and strokes his forehead.

"Alice loved you very much . . ."

"Why did you send me those messages?"

Luciana opens the nightstand drawer. Slowly she takes something out. A phone.

Alice's.

"Take it. She wanted to tell you everything."

The charger port is identical to his, now all he has to do is turn it on.

"Will Sandro be back soon?" Luciana asks him.

"He had an accident, but as I told you, I'll take care of things. As soon as there is any news, I'll make sure you know."

"Sandro takes care of me every night."

Enrico tries to find something to add, but he can't come up with anything. Luciana spares him the embarrassment by turning back to the TV. The star of a soap opera is making a fool of himself trying to dance a tango.

"I'll come back to tell you about Sandro," he says.

But Luciana doesn't respond. She has returned to her world.

Enrico leaves the room and goes downstairs. Opens the door and hurries to the car. He gets in. He lifts up the armrest and finds a charger for the cigarette lighter. He inserts the jack. The phone turns on. There's no PIN, because Alice was always forgetting things like that and deactivated it.

The messages are saved in the phone memory.

They are still there.

Enrico starts to read.

Ten

The Alfa may have a few years on it, but some things improve with age. And Frank's voice gliding on velvet in "Fly Me to the Moon" is proof of that.

Steely Gloria had already decided to go even before reading her granddaughter's message. Because she knew they needed her.

Those two still haven't learned how to get themselves out of trouble, him in particular, a loser, a pathetic waste. He's been the worst misfortune that could have happened to her daughter and her grandchildren. A little boy who can't manage to keep his dick in his shorts sooner or later becomes a problem. And Maurizio Germano has always been a problem. Except that, unlike so many other problems that in some way can be resolved or forgotten, he is still a living disaster. With that suntan meant for a guy of twenty and the attitude of an ambitious go-getter, when all he's built is a real-estate agency with only one employee, whom he must surely have fucked behind the desk, because little boys like that are so dismally predictable. So many times she's watched him, unnoticed. So many times she's sat in the car, parked on the street, to see Chiara grow up and become the young woman she is now.

She has always looked out for them.

By the time it starts to rain, Gloria is already at the exit of the Aurelia. She hopes that Chiara isn't getting drenched. She still doesn't know exactly what happened, but it's obvious that those two have failed to manage even one single daughter. And that one would do well to leave too. Follow her sister and go someplace where she can be free of the pathetic burden her parents have become. They messed her up but good, that girl. And as usual it will be up to Steely Gloria to fix everything. Fortunately, some things age well.

Why isn't Margherita answering? Chiara left her another message, this time on Facebook. But the only notifications on her cell phone are the three calls from her mother, which she hasn't answered. She doesn't feel like talking to her and admitting that she was right about Gibo; she doesn't want to talk to her after seeing her father in that situation; and she especially doesn't want to explain why she contacted her grandmother. She doesn't know if she hates her mother or feels sorry for her, and until she figures it out, she won't answer the phone. She wrote Margherita and told her she wanted to escape from there. But she didn't tell her about that slut from the beauty salon. She only told her that something strange is going on at home, that they're all very worried about something that seems to have to do with the death of that girl, Alice. That it's just what you'd expect from people who are off their rockers. She didn't tell her about her grandmother. *But what the fuck, Marghe, you could have answered.* So she writes about her now, how Gloria is the only one there for her. She types the last message a little angrily.

I'm waiting for grandma. Maybe with her I can talk a little.

As soon as she sends it, a thunder clap silences everyone and the light in the station bar flickers, as if it were going to go out at any moment. The sound of the pelting rain is stronger now. And the guys speaking an incomprehensible Eastern European language start laughing after being struck dumb by the violence of the storm. They're probably saying how lucky they are to be in here drinking that crappy grappa and good thing there's that game to watch; though here, it seems, nobody gives a damn about it. Chiara doesn't even notice when one of them comes over to her.

"Ciao, how come you're all alone?" he asks her. He smiles. He has white teeth and dark eyes. His haircut looks like crap and is combed with a part on one side, as if he were going to Communion. "Want a glass to warm up a bit?" he asks, setting one down on the table.

Chiara smiles and takes the glass. She looks at the others, who raise theirs in a toast. She drinks it all in one gulp. Her throat burns, but the feeling it leaves isn't bad. That stuff really can warm you up.

"Thanks, just what I needed."

"If you need another, we're over there."

The guy goes back to the table with his friends, who laugh, slap him on the back, and say something dirty that, as only males can do, makes even such a nice gesture seem vulgar. Chiara picks up the glass and goes over to their table. The guy nudges the one sitting next to him, who immediately jumps up to make room for her and goes to look for another chair.

"I could use another," Chiara says, holding out the glass.

And a second bottle appears on the table.

Maurizio enters the house. He's soaking wet. He's still dabbing his forehead with the cloth used to wipe the car windows. He drops the keys in the plate. Betti is in the living room, sitting at the table with the cordless and cell phones in front of her.

"What are you doing?" Maurizio asks her.

"Chiara isn't answering."

"Isn't she with Gloria?"

"That's the point."

"She'll bring her home."

"I don't want you to speak to her."

"Why not?"

Betti explodes and slams her hands on the table.

"Fuck! How can you ask that?"

She looks up and only now realizes that Maurizio is dabbing at his forehead. "What happened to you?"

"Got in a scrape."

The druggie, that Bastiani, is in the ambulance. Apparently, he's okay. The doctor says he only has a few superficial fractures. They'll take him to the ER to make sure, but the reason he said those ridiculous things isn't a concussion, but a hearty dose of heroin that is still merrily circulating in his brain. Enzo listens to him as he watches Ekaterina's long, slim fingers tending to the patient. Maybe he could take advantage of the moment to ask her if . . .

"Are you doing okay?" the doctor asks him.

Enzo thinks about it.

"Sometimes I have a pain here," he says, pointing to his left elbow.

"I meant tonight, is everything all right with you?"

"Tonight it's not bothering me, it does occasionally, when the weather changes."

"Okay then, we're off."

The doctor climbs in. The door is about to close. Enzo has to speak to her. The door is almost shut. Yes, he has to speak to her. Say something to her. It's closing. *I'll tell her that . . .* Closed.

The ambulance leaves.

Shit.

"Are you the one who called for assistance?"

Enzo turns.

The carabinieri.

"I should have said something to her, shit."

"Sorry, what's that?"

McClane is standing in the rain. He takes off his cap and wipes his face. *Bad night, Lieutenant.* But it's not so bad when it rains. You don't see this shitty town's housing complexes, and you can pretend that there are skyscrapers and streets full of cars under that downpour. And there's always a scene with a policeman in the rain. The cop beside him hands him a cup of coffee. *In the end, it's a dirty job. But someone has to do it, Central.*

"Did you hear me? Are you the one who called for assistance?"

"Affirmative, agent."

"I'm not an agent, I'm a police officer. See the uniform?"

Assholes.

◆ ◆ ◆

"You just need to rest," says Alice, who is sitting beside him.

Sandro looks around and doesn't recognize the room he's in. It's all white, and it looks like a spaceship. That guy in the documentary who said he was abducted by aliens described a similar place.

"Just rest," Alice says again.

Sometimes a young woman whom he doesn't know is superimposed on her. She has blonde hair and pale-blue eyes. She speaks with a strange accent that comes and goes. She looks at him for a few seconds, then Alice returns.

"You'll see, everything will be all right," says one of the two of them.

"Are you an idiot?"

Betti has a vein on her neck that sometimes swells and looks horrible. It usually does that when she's angry. Maybe it pumps the blood to her brain.

"I was just trying to find that fucking phone."

"And if he saw you?"

"He didn't see me! Don't you listen to me when I talk?"

"How do you know he didn't see you?"

"Betti, for Chrissake, I told you he didn't see me!"

"But the phone wasn't there?"

"No, goddammit. That shitty phone wasn't there."

"Okay, but then . . ."

The doorbell. They plunge into silence and look into each other's eyes. It's clear who it is. They both know. Betti goes to the window. Just to confirm, merely a formality. Because it's him. She knows it even before she sees him. Even before she sees his profile in the rain. Standing in front of their gate.

"It's him," she says.

"Oh shit."

"Maybe he just wants to talk."

"Yeah sure, it seems like just the perfect evening," says Maurizio. "He definitely came to relive some old memories."

"Try to stay calm and fix yourself up."

"I have a cut on my forehead. How the fuck do you expect me to fix myself up?"

"Make up a story then."

"You know what I'll do if . . ."

"Stop it!" The vein is pulsing even harder. "I have to open the door."

Betti turns the knob and presses the button for the small gate. Enrico walks slowly. He doesn't seem to care about the rain. He climbs the steps. His eyes are wide open, as if he were possessed by a demon. He doesn't say a word. He goes inside. Maurizio and Betti just stare at him, waiting for him to say something. But he doesn't speak. He walks slowly into the hall, toward the living room. He leaves a trail of mud in his wake. Betti closes the front door and follows him. Maurizio keeps dabbing at his cut. Enrico stands beside the coffee table. He's facing the window. His back to them. The curtain does not allow them to see his face reflected in the glass. He remains silent.

"Enrico?" Betti says.

He doesn't answer. He reaches into his pocket. He takes something out and sets it on the table.

Alice's phone.

Each glass of grappa burns less, while continuing to deliver that nice warm feeling. Chiara has almost forgotten about everything else. About Gibo, the beautician, her parents who seem to have a big problem with Enrico. Staying here with Peter and the other guys wouldn't be so bad. Some are from Bulgaria, some from Ukraine, and one from Moldova. They work at a construction site. They're even working tomorrow, which is Sunday. The sooner they finish the better, because not one among them is a legal employee. They sleep in a warehouse.

And then the door opens.

Black trench coat belted at the waist, red purse on her arm. Her silver hair gathered up in a chignon. The signature pearls on her ears and around her neck.

Gloria closes her umbrella and smiles at Chiara.

Eleven

The rain beating against the windowpanes is the only sound in Maurizio and Betti Germano's living room.

Enrico still has his back to them. He's opened the curtain and is staring out the window. The almond tree is now bare. That evening, ten years ago, in that garden, it was in bloom. He was dancing with Betti, Alice was with them. A party, with colored paper plates, colored paper cups, music.

A few hours later Alice would be killed and his life would be plunged into a place he would never climb out of. A crevasse, a well. An abyss. For years he would wonder if he should seek help from his friends. If he should go back and ask them to lighten that load. His friends.

"Maybe it's time you said something," Betti says.

Enrico waits. He's sopping wet. A puddle of water has formed around him on the living room floor. Rain lashes the windows.

"The first thing I asked myself was whether you knew about it." He brushes the glass with wet fingers. "But you always know everything, don't you, Betti? So you knew about that too. And you didn't tell me."

"If anyone should have told you . . ." Maurizio tries to say.

"It certainly wasn't you," Enrico cuts him off. He still has his back turned. "According to what's in those texts, it seems Alice was the only one who wanted to tell me." He turns around finally. His face is strained, tense. "Only I argued with her. I didn't even give her a chance to speak."

"It's not your fault if . . ." Maurizio tries again.

"The second thing I wondered is how the hell could you, Maurizio, write her those messages and then look me in the eye. All those 'I love you,' all those 'I can't live without you,' all those good intentions to drop everything and go away with her, as if you were a couple of kids running off for the weekend. And I wondered, reading that crap, if you seriously meant it. If you really believed it or were only bullshitting Alice the way you've bullshitted me and everyone around you your whole shitty fucking life."

Thunder. The pounding rain. Betti has sat down. She looks defeated, crushed by a weight she can no longer bear. Maurizio is standing there, holding the cloth to his head and dabbing at the cut. Enrico looks at the bloodstained cloth.

"The security guard says Sandro is okay and that he's convinced he was hit by the car because he'd forgotten to set the hand brake. Sandro told him that for a moment he thought he saw someone in the car. But he wasn't lucid, he had too much heroin in his body and kept seeing things that weren't there. While they were taking him to the hospital, he kept talking to someone, so he must have been certain he'd had another hallucination. I wonder why I'm not so sure, Maurizio."

The rain. Pounding.

"But he didn't have it, the phone," Enrico continues. "His mother had it. Imagine that? It was Luciana who sent me those messages."

The rain. Beating down.

Enrico goes over to Betti.

"You're silent, Betti. Usually you're not. Usually you always have something to say. I know what you're waiting for. I know you see where I'm going. What the third thing I wondered about is. Am I right? Because you knew about that too. It's clear now. And I get the feeling you stayed with him despite everything, just to cover up what happened. Because I know that in some way it concerns you. Nothing to say? Still not time to talk? Fine. I'll go on then. Just think, Sandro's mother, who kept this phone with her for all these years, convinced that I alone should read the truth about Alice and Maurizio, didn't understand the most important thing. Because she didn't know who Mr. Toby was."

The rain. Beating down.

"It's one of the messages that was received," Enrico says, picking up the phone and scrolling through the menus. "You should recognize it, Maurizio, you sent it. That's why you asked me those things about her phone, right? That's why you were worried that someone might have it, isn't it? Go ahead, read it if you don't remember." He hands him the phone.

"I remember it."

"Then would you kindly read it to all of us?"

Maurizio's eyes are fixed on the text.

"Is there a problem? Something you don't understand that keeps you from reading it?"

"No. It's that . . . Betti, do you want . . ."

"Read it," Enrico orders him.

"I . . ."

"Read the message," Betti says.

"'You left Mr. Toby in the bathroom, when you did that psycho number. I'll bring him to you tomorrow. I love you.'"

"Mr. Toby," Enrico says with enthusiasm, as if he had just made a sensational discovery. "The very one. Alice's turtle-shaped pendant. The same one Giancarlo told the police he'd found the Half-Wit holding, which was considered proof that the dumb beast, the monster, had attacked Alice that night in the woods."

Rain. Beating. Down.

"And there it is, the third thing I wondered as I read the messages preserved in the memory of her phone. How is it possible that Mr. Toby was teleported, all by himself, from your bathroom, where Alice was the night of the party, the night she was killed, to the Half-Wit's house? Because if he didn't get there by himself, then it would mean that someone had to have brought him there. Or would anyone like to tell me that the Half-Wit suddenly left the woods and came out here to take it, out of the blue, for no fucking reason? And since you, my dear friend Maurizio who always brought me focaccias, knew where that pendant was, because you sent that message while Alice was probably still in the car with me, one would think that it was you who brought him there. But that doesn't make sense, does it? Why would you have done that?"

"That's enough," Betti breaks in. "Maurizio had an affair with Alice and I knew about it. Like I've always known about his affairs. But if you think he killed her because she wanted to leave him, or that I killed her because he wanted to leave me, then you're wrong, Enrico. That's not how things went."

"How then, Betti? You have to tell me, it affects me too. For ten years it's affected me."

"I know."

"I need a drink," says Maurizio. He goes over to a cabinet, takes a glass, fills it halfway, and downs it. "Want some, Erri?"

"Pour a glass for everyone," Betti says.

"He's a shit, definitely a shit. But she at times is really hard to take."

Chiara is in the car with her grandmother. Gloria arrived shortly after Chiara texted her, since she had already left. Because, evidently, she's better than others at being able to know when someone needs her. Chiara finally manages to get it all out. They took a drive, just to break the ice, after Gloria found her at the bar. Her grandmother told her that she smelled of grappa. Chiara rolled the window down to clear the air, but the rain soaked her so she rolled it back up. Finally, Gloria pulled over on Chiara's street. Nearby there's a small park with swings where Chiara always went with her father when she was little. *It would be nice to sit there in the rain, swinging back and forth,* Chiara thought.

"How can anyone be around her without feeling oppressed by her sadness?" Chiara said to her grandmother. "She's always like that, always worried, always obsessive. It's as if there was a cloud over our house. The air is always so heavy that it's normal to want to get away. So why won't they let me go, like they let Margherita leave? She got out of there. And now I don't know why she will not even answer me anymore."

"What did you tell her?"

"I wanted to know if she at least knew what was going on. Why everything has to be so complicated and difficult. Why can't we ever talk about you, for example? Why do I have to spend a shitty night like this, and believe me it was really shitty, and not feel like going home even under these circumstances? I had a fight with my boyfriend, who apparently wasn't even *my* boyfriend, and the thing that bugs me the most is to have to admit it to her. And him, that shit, with the beautician, can you imagine? That's why he's always so tan. How pathetic. Should I tell her? At the very least she'll have an attack of nerves and I don't want to be there alone with her when she has a meltdown. Why doesn't anybody care about my nerves?"

"Is that why you reached out to me?"

"I didn't know who to call, okay?"

"I don't mean tonight. You reached out to me because you realized that there's something wrong in your family and you thought I could help you understand what it is."

"Yeah."

"You see, this has been a topic of much disagreement between me and your mother."

"Then you talk to each other?"

"It would be more correct to say that I turn up, sometimes."

"She says you always want things done your way, that she keeps you away from us because otherwise we'd all have to do what you say. That you're intrusive and you want to teach her how to manage her family. That's why she doesn't want you around."

"She's wrong about a lot of things, Chiara. She keeps getting it wrong. She's wrong to think she can protect you that way, because she doesn't understand that by doing so she drives you away. She's wrong to stay with him, because he's nothing but a shit, as you say, a pathetic loser. And she did the wrong thing with your sister. She shouldn't have split you up. You're part of this family; you should have known everything from the start."

Gloria seems lost in thought as she talks.

"What should I have known?"

"What's that?"

"You said I should have known from the start. Known what?"

"I'm not the one who should tell you; they'd never forgive me."

"She won't tell me, she never tells me anything. All she does is find fault with me, tell me what to do. What should I know?"

"It's not right for me to be the one to tell you."

"Tell me *what*?"

"It should . . ."

"Grandma, if you don't tell me I'm getting out of this car and, like her, I swear I won't ever speak to you again."

Gloria seems to count the raindrops falling on the Alfa's windshield. Then she looks at Chiara.

"What the hell, you should have known a long time ago. After all, you were there that night too."

"What night, Grandma? What are you talking about? Where was I too?"

Gloria opens the glove compartment and takes out a pack of cigarettes. She offers one to Chiara and lights up. She lowers the window a crack to let the smoke out.

Chiara waits for what's coming.

"Do you remember anything about the day that girl, Alice Bastiani, was killed?"

"Margherita and I were with you. You took us to the movies, in Rome."

"Your parents were having a party at their house. So that afternoon I came by to pick you up. I got to town, drove to the bar. You two were there waiting for me. Margherita was confused, angry. She'd found out about something that upset her, in much the same way that you found out tonight. Your father, Chiara. He's always been the problem. Margherita had discovered that he was secretly seeing someone else. And that he'd told the girl he wanted to leave his family to go away with her. She'd learned about it by accident and had spoken to me about it. She didn't know what to do about your mother. Just like you. She was really afraid that your father would leave you. That he would abandon you. That he preferred that other girl to all of you. Margherita was a delightful, sunny girl. She knew nothing about hatred. But it was that girl who made her come to know it. The girl who was going to take your father away."

PART FOUR

AT THE END OF THE NIGHT

One

Chiara is asleep in the car seat in back. Betti had insisted she have one installed and Gloria had eventually given in, even if that childish accessory didn't match the Alfa's style. And style is an important element in life. She'd picked up the girls and brought them to Rome. An afternoon of shopping and then a movie, at Warner Village—she and Chiara an animated feature with a lot of little animals talking and dancing, Margherita a film about a madman slaughtering a group of kids with a chainsaw. Burgers, fries, a stroll through the bookstore, and a few games at the arcade, then back to the car. It's not the long drive that bothers Gloria. Of course not. It's the strange melancholy surrounding Margherita that worries her. She isn't talking much, and she's withdrawn into herself with those earbuds stuck in her ears. It's clear she's going through a bad period. For teenagers, it's the norm. Margherita is a beautiful girl. More beautiful than her mother. Beautiful as only Gloria, in her day, was. The boys will go crazy over her, that's for sure. But males have the unfortunate quality of being mentally deficient. So as soon as Chiara falls asleep in that silly seat, Gloria decides to try and put the girl at ease. And it works. Margherita tells her what's been bothering her.

She tells her about her father. She tells her about that girl. Will he really leave them? Will he leave them all for her? Why couldn't she find someone else? Wasn't that guy from Rome enough for her? He's loaded and could give her anything she wants, but no. She wants Margherita's father. She knows her kind, that spoiled bitch. She wants it all, especially what belongs to others.

"You mustn't talk like that," Gloria says.

"Who cares? Who can hear me now?"

"I hear you, and I don't like you talking that way. Only foolish girls talk that vulgar. You're not one of them."

"Yeah, but apparently, he prefers one of them to all of us."

Gloria would like to tell her that her father is an idiot, nothing but a pathetic loser, as Gloria calls him, and that he has always been a big problem. She'd like to tell her that she'd always hoped her daughter would choose someone else, Enrico for example. A well-mannered young man, from a good family. Someone she'd always gotten on well with but who, for some reason, had never stepped forward that way. For a time she'd thought he was one of those.

"He won't do it," Gloria says.

"How do you know? He told her he wants to leave. I heard him talking to her on the phone. I read the messages they send each other. He really wants to go away with her. I don't care if in the end he won't. He'd like to, that's what matters. He's sick of his life with us."

"It's because of that girl." That's not true, she knows, it's because he's an idiot. But for tonight it will do.

"That bitch."

"What did I tell you?"

"So tell me another word I can use that has the same meaning. Because you can use all the words you want, but that's what she is. Some people could use a lesson."

"What kind of lesson?"

"I don't know, but what she's doing isn't right."

"She's not doing it on her own." *Look, Margherita, try to understand that your father is an idiot, and that he's not even worth it.*

"It's all her fault. If you know how to do it, men can be wrapped around your little finger."

"That's true."

"And she sure knows how. And then she complains if someone goes after her."

"What do you mean?"

"Today at the bar, she was there too. I don't even know how I managed not to smack her, that bitch . . ."

"Again?"

"She's a bitch and that's all there is to it. Anyway, while I was waiting for you I went to the bathroom, because I couldn't stand to watch her there with Mom talking to her and inviting her to dinner. Sometimes it seems like Mom really doesn't want to see certain things and pretends not to notice. It was humiliating, you know? So I went to the bathroom so I wouldn't lose it. And while I was there, I heard the bitch talking with her brother. Apparently, the Half-Wit . . . You know who I mean? That guy in town who's not right in the head? Anyway, he follows her. He bothers her, the poor thing. Maybe she rubbed up against him like a cat in heat just to enjoy making him get hard . . ."

"Margherita!"

"That's what girls like her do. Anyway, it seems he must have done something, he must have annoyed her, so she asked her brother to set him straight. That fascist bully, I can just imagine . . . Anyhow, it seems that the Half-Wit was actually about to jump her. And that's just what she deserves. Girls like her should end up just like that . . . You always play this stuff on the stereo?"

"'This stuff'? Honey, that's Frank and 'Fly Me to the Moon.'"

They're about to pass the Bastiani farmhouse. You can see it from the road. Who knows if Alice is already back, Gloria wonders. Who knows what she did tonight. She has her mother's crazy genes. Luciana in her day used to have quite a good time too before Giancarlo. Really hard to understand how someone like him, one of the few men with a brain around here, went and got mixed up with her. The result couldn't have been anything but Alice, in the end.

They drive by the house and continue along the provincial road to Carrubo.

"What's that over there?" Margherita says, peering up ahead.

"Someone's there," says Gloria, a moment before realizing who it is.

"Grandma, it's her!"

The bitch is actually coming out of the woods. She'd been hiding. And, if she were hiding, it means she wasn't with Enrico. It means she had something to hide. Does she really think she can destroy Gloria's family? Does she really think she can steal the husband of Gloria's daughter? And what if Maurizio is there? Maybe the girl would realize that he's just a sorry asshole.

"So then, tonight we make a scene," Gloria says.

"What do you mean? You want to stop and talk to her?"

"If we wait for your mother to do it, it'll never happen."

Margherita doesn't say a word. Gloria's Alfa draws near the girl, who is now heading back into the woods. Maybe she was waiting for someone else. The bitch.

Gloria stops the car and gets out. Margherita follows her.

"Expecting someone?" Gloria asks her.

"I'm waiting for my brother, why?" The Bastiani girl has always had that haughty attitude that gets on her nerves.

"You know why, bitch."

Margherita turns to her grandmother. Gloria smiles at her.

"What are you talking about?"

"You want to pretend there's nothing going on? See, it's okay for my daughter to pretend not to notice, but not for me."

"What do you mean?"

"She's talking about my father, bitch." Margherita takes a step toward her.

Alice is dumbfounded, taken by surprise. She can't seem to find the right words.

"It's all straightened out with Maurizio, it's . . . it's over," she stammers.

Her voice is unsure. It's clear she's lying. Women like her always lie. Margherita doesn't know the whole story. For example, she doesn't know that Betti has already discovered what was going on between them. But she doesn't have the strength to defend what's hers, it always falls to her mother to take care of it.

"Anyway, what do you want from me? If you have something to say, go tell him. Call me a bitch one more time, and you'll be in big trouble."

"*We'll* be in trouble?" Gloria's eyes are now blazing like torches. "And what trouble would we be in? Tell us."

"I'll report you, for threatening me. Then we'll all be disgraced. After all, I have nothing to lose anymore."

"Oh no, you shouldn't have said that." Gloria goes up to her. "You're not reporting anyone, you're not saying a damn thing."

"Or what, Gloria. Huh? Or what? Let's hear it. Will you offer me money too? See, Margherita, maybe you don't know it, but that's how your grandmother settles things. Do you know she offered your father money to leave?"

"Stop it!" Gloria is close beside her now. That's not a story that Margherita should hear. How did that slut know about it?

"And that's not all. Make her tell you what she suggested to your mother when she got pregnant with you. Go ahead, Gloria, why don't you . . ."

A sharp thump. Somehow that rock had appeared in Gloria's hand. Alice slumps to the ground. Margherita turns to her.

"Grandma . . . what . . . what did you do?"

Gloria keeps staring at Alice. She's not moving.

"Oh my God, Grandma . . . what . . ."

"Stay calm."

Gloria bends down. Leans close to the bitch's face. *You made Maurizio tell you that too? You were really about to put your foot in it. Next time you'll think twice.*

"Grandma, is she alive?"

Margherita's voice comes from a distance. Gloria can't seem to understand what she's asking at first. The problem is "next time." There's unlikely to be one.

"Is she alive?"

Now the voice is closer. The distance has shrunk. Everything is back to normal. Everything except Alice, lifeless, stretched out in front of her. No "next time." She's dead. Just as well.

"No, she's not alive."

"Shit, Grandma . . ." Margherita bursts into tears. "Oh God, what did you do? You killed her. Oh my God . . ."

"Calm down," Gloria says, standing up. "We have to keep calm now." She looks around, picks up the blood-smeared rock. "Let's go."

"Where?"

"Away from here. You want us to ruin our lives over this little tramp?"

"But . . ." The girl is distraught, she needs time. She starts to approach the dead body, but she's terrified.

"She was expecting her brother, we have to get out of here before he comes. We'll come up with something. We'll figure out what to do."

"I . . ."

"Let's go, come on. I'm certainly not going to get into hot water over this bitch. Understand? At this point everyone has to do their part. Now that we're free of her, everything will go back to the way it was before. Wasn't that what you wanted? Wasn't that what we all wanted? It happened. And now all we can do is leave here and forget about it. And everything will fall back into place."

Chiara is sleeping the way only children can. Dead to the world, her head lolling to one side. Margherita, however, is cold. She put Gloria's trench coat over her shoulders. She keeps looking through the window and crying.

Gloria stops near a stream. She takes the rock and gets out of the car, but then she hesitates. The stream is just along the road. What if the police were to find the rock? How many whodunnits had she seen that were solved that way? Could fragments of Alice's skull have been left on the rock? Could DNA traces remain despite the water? She has to dump it a distance away, farther from the road. She gets back in the car and they set off again.

"Grandma . . ."

"What is it, sweetheart?"

"What was she about to say?"

"Listen to me, Margherita. You won't believe a word that bitch said, will you? Nothing but lies came out of that mouth. Forget it."

"What do we do now?" Margherita asks. She's crying, trembling. She's in shock.

"We take our time, we decide."

"What is there to decide?"

"Whether to tell your parents, for instance."

"I want to tell them."

"Are you sure?"

"Yes."

"All right, that's settled."

It would have been much better to avoid it, but the girl would have told them anyway. Maybe not right away, but sooner or later the truth would have come out. And the risk that it might come out in the wrong way and at the wrong time is too great.

So, family meeting.

When they get home, Maurizio and Betti are just about done tidying up after the party.

As soon as they enter, Margherita runs to her mother. Sobbing, she hugs her. Betti looks at her mother to find out what happened to the girl. Gloria is standing in front of the door with Chiara, still sleeping, in her arms.

"We need to talk."

Two

"I should have called the police," Betti says.

Enrico is sitting next to her, the sound of rain, still, on the living room windows. Maurizio is lying on the couch with a glass of scotch resting on his stomach and a clean cloth on his wound.

"But it was my mother. And Margherita was with her. Can you understand? So I made a decision. Maurizio told me about the message he had sent to Alice, that she had left that pendant in the bathroom, and my mother came up with the idea, because Margherita had told her that she heard Alice telling Sandro that the Half-Wit was bothering her. I don't know what we were thinking, maybe it was just to buy time. I never meant for him to end up like that. All it took was that pendant and Giancarlo's strange, incomprehensible story about the Half-Wit's confession and the case was closed. And if you're wondering, I was the one who brought the pendant there. Maurizio waited for me in the car. I slipped into the woods and started walking. But first there was something else I had to do. I turned toward the bend. And I found her. She was lying there. I wanted to move her body closer to the Half-Wit's house. I had started thinking like a murderer. It seems insane when I think about it now. But I thought that if the body were nearby, it would corroborate the story that it had been him and I would be able to save my family. That's understandable, isn't it, Enrico? Do you see

that I did everything to save my family? It was my duty. So I picked up
Alice's body and carried it near the Half-Wit's house. Just a short time
earlier we had hugged. When you both arrived at the party, she'd come
over to me and hugged me tighter than usual. And at that moment,
as I was hauling her through the woods, we were hugging again. I was
exhausted, but I was driven by a crazy rush of adrenaline. Almost a feeling of well-being. And you know why I did it? You know why I wanted
to do it *myself*? This is the most absurd part. I didn't want Maurizio to
touch her again. I didn't want him to have a chance to say good-bye
to her. I wouldn't grant him that moment. But when I got close to the
Half-Wit's house, I saw lights cutting through the woods from the other
direction, near the bend. So I left Alice's body on the ground, picked up
a stone, wrapped the necklace with the pendant around it, and threw
it toward the Half-Wit's house, hoping they'd find it there. I was so . . .
I know it's terrible, but I felt so *satisfied*. I had done it all by myself. I
had fixed everything. It seemed like a game. The plot of a TV detective story, like those *Columbo* episodes, when you follow the killer at
the beginning as he erases the evidence and constructs an alibi for his
perfect murder. As you can see, we made mistakes all along the line. We
thought we were saving our family, and instead we destroyed all that
was left of it. We all became accessories to a murder. Unintentionally,
my mother says. But, in the end, even I don't believe it. Afterward
Margherita couldn't take it anymore. We had to send her away, because
she was likely to have a fit of hysteria every time she passed those woods.
I didn't know what to do with her. You can understand that at that point
we were all so compromised. I waited until she calmed down a little,
we talked about a school in England. She liked the idea. For years I
expected a call from a teacher: 'Ma'am, we have to speak to you about
your daughter, and a murder.' But the years passed and nothing happened. I deluded myself that time would fix everything. Instead, it's as if
time had stopped that night. And I relive it every time I close my eyes.
I see Alice walking over to greet me. I think about what we did. It's like

carrying a black hole inside me that swallows up everything else. You're left with nothing. You remain imprisoned by a secret. Your life belongs to it. And you let it consume you, day after day, as it robs a piece of you for every lie that you are forced to tell. What else can a murderer do when he gets away with it? When nobody finds out about him? If after the murder the authorities, unlike Lieutenant Columbo, don't ask too many questions and accept a different version of what happened, and no one even remotely considers the fact that things may have gone differently? If no one looks for the murderer, if no one figures it out? If no one suspects? And then one day you show up and discover the only evidence that we left behind. We were sure we had disposed of that too. When I left Alice's body near the Half-Wit's house, I took her phone, shattered it, and threw it in the trash. That was my mistake, Enrico. It took ten years for it to come out, but, in the end, it did. Apparently, that was the wrong phone. And now I don't know what else to tell you. So pick up that phone and go home. It's up to you to decide now. It's a weight that from this moment on I will no longer have to carry."

Three

"Are you afraid?"

"A little."

Gloria has just finished the story. They're riding in the same car, but this time Chiara isn't sitting in the back, in a car seat. She's sitting right where her sister was that night.

"You shouldn't be, of any of us. You're the only one who had nothing to do with it."

"I shouldn't be? My entire family is an accessory to the murder that everyone in this lousy town talks about, and I shouldn't be scared?"

"Chiara . . ."

"Never mind 'Chiara,' fucking shit, Grandma. Just when were you thinking of telling me?"

"You shouldn't . . ."

"Don't tell me what I should do. It seems you're not the best person to do that."

"Now calm down."

"No, I'm not going to calm down. And I'm scared. Tell me, have you bumped off anyone else in the meantime?"

"What are you talking about?"

"I don't know, maybe someone who found out about you . . ."

"Chiara . . ."

"Jesusfuckingchrist, stop saying 'Chiara, Chiara,' fuck that."

"I told you it was an accident, no one meant . . ."

"And that other bitch who went away and has been feeding me a load of crap for ten years."

"We did it to protect you."

"That's bullshit."

"And stop talking like that. I decided to tell you everything, but if that's the way you're going to react, it means I shouldn't have told you. That your mother was right not to want to tell you."

The girl is breathing hard. She's different from her sister. It's anger that drives her, not fear. The thought of having to admit her mother was right was a decisive factor. She's stubborn. Obstinate. She's the last link in the family and in this entire story. And she could be the strongest. The most solid. Just what's needed most now.

Gloria takes the umbrella.

"Where are you going?" Chiara asks.

"You said the car parked over there is Enrico's."

"Yeah, so?"

"I'm going to go say hello to him and tell your parents that you and I had a little chat. It's right that you speak with them now, and whatever happens next should concern them and not me."

"I . . ."

"You have to calm down. The worst decisions are those made in the heat of the moment. Stay here, try to work through your feelings. Right now you're too shaken. Everything will seem clear and simple once things settle down. Wait for me here."

Gloria opens the umbrella and steps out. She didn't hear Chiara mutter "settle my ass" as soon as the door closed.

Gloria approaches her daughter's house down the street. The light in the living room is on. She has no intention of ringing the bell. She wants to see what's going on. She peers through the window and can make out Enrico. He's sitting next to Betti. She's talking. He's staring at an empty glass. Gloria moves close to the door and presses her ear against it.

Betti goes on, telling him everything that happened. That idiot. Gloria stands there listening. Her daughter keeps talking, all you hear is her voice. She pictures Enrico sitting beside her, listening. She got there too late. If she had arrived before him, she could have convinced Betti to tell a different story. Why tell him everything now? He's not a member of the family. He might have been. And if he had been, this whole mess would never have happened. Because Enrico is different from Maurizio. Enrico is someone who is unable to lie. And now that could be a huge problem.

"So pick up that phone and go home. It's up to you to decide now. It's a weight that from this moment on I will no longer have to carry."

Betti must have lost her mind. The stress must have gotten to her. Putting their fate in the hands of an outsider. Imagine. After all they'd done up to now. And that insignificant, useless, pathetic asshole Maurizio lies there without saying a word. Would it really have been so difficult to make up a story to tell him? They were talking about a phone. A phone.

Dear God, does it make sense to confess everything over a phone? Couldn't they come up with some excuse, a fabrication, something to explain the phone? Do I always have to take care of everything? Can't they resolve anything without me? Must I always be the one to pick up the pieces? Is it conceivable that all the men we've had in our lives have always been a problem? Fortunately, the children are girls. And I must be present, from now on, to make sure they keep their guard up. To make sure they both know that all men are deceitful assholes like their father. And that those who aren't, and they are few indeed, are likely to become a worse problem. Because the only thing that really matters is family. There are no principles that count more than that. Defending the family should be one's main obligation. Because everything is founded on the family. And it's women who must sustain it, because men, after having done their reproductive duty, only serve to create problems. And then they just get old, they piss their pants, and their women have to clean up after them. There are insects that kill the male after mating. Nature knows what needs to be done. God took care of Alfredo, a nice heart attack and off he went. Of course, I gave him a hand. I realized he was in difficulty, that he had slumped to the floor, and I went to the movies. There was a good film playing too. And when I came back, he had relieved us of his presence. Now, sooner or later, we'll have to see to Maurizio.

Gloria walks quickly back to the Alfa and opens the door. Chiara is still there. Good.

"Well?" her granddaughter asks.

"So go home. I explained it all and everything is fine."

"You let Mom know you told me?"

"Of course."

"And?"

"She got very angry with me, as she usually does. But Enrico is with her, and he was always able to make her feel better."

"You told him everything too?"

"Of course not. I spoke with Betti in the kitchen. Certain things mustn't leave the family, remember that."

"What about you? Are you going back to your house?"

"Yes, I'm going now. Will you come and see me again?"

"I don't know. I have to think about it."

"Good, an excellent response. As I told you, never make hasty decisions."

Chiara opens the door.

"Wait a minute," Gloria says. "Maybe when it's not raining so hard."

A few minutes go by in silence, until Gloria sees the door of the house open.

"Okay, Chiara, maybe you'd better go. You wouldn't want to stay here all night. Take the umbrella, pull your hood up, and try to make a run for it."

"You could drive me up to the door . . ."

"I'm not going that way. I'm turning around here. I told your mother I changed cars, that I have one that doesn't go as fast now. Let's not let her see that it's not true."

Chiara takes the umbrella, opens the door, and gets out.

It's raining cats and dogs. She closes the Alfa's door behind her. What a god-awful night. There are so many things she has to tell her mother. Best to start with Gibo. Because now, suddenly, she feels like telling her about that too. She wants to sit on the bed with a nice hot cup of Nesquik and tell her everything. And tomorrow Margherita. That's why her sister wasn't answering. Now she can though. Now they can talk about everything. No more secrets, no more silence, no more skeletons in the closet. *Even so, I'm still a little pissed at her,* Chiara thinks. *In fact, I'm still a little pissed at all of them.*

Here comes Enrico. Opening the gate. He's leaving.

Chiara wants to say hello to him. Maybe one of these days they can meet up again and have lunch together. She walks faster to catch up with him. He hasn't seen her. His car is parked across the street, and he steps down from the sidewalk to cross over. He doesn't seem to be in a hurry. He doesn't seem to care about the rain.

The roar of the Alfa comes out of nowhere. Her grandmother didn't turn around, she didn't go back the way she said. She's heading this way, toward her parents' house, toward Enrico. The wall of water raised by the car as it speeds by hits Chiara squarely and washes over her. When she opens her eyes again, Enrico is no longer in the street.

All she sees is the Alfa, a missile hurtling down the street and then suddenly gliding, like an ice skater.

The oil slick.

Gloria had been going so fast she hadn't seen the sign. In technical terms—the same terms the police will use in the course of their investigation, the same terms they'll use when they reach the scene of what will be recorded as a tragic accident resulting from bad weather and poor maintenance on the part of the refinery—one would say that "the car lost traction due to an oil spill." Gloria's Alfa kicks up jets of water, out of control. It starts spinning around like a centrifugal clothes dryer and then flips over, once, twice, three times. Finally, it crashes into a tree and all its lights come on at the same time. Red ones, yellow ones, blinkers and headlights. And it remains there, motionless, lighting up the whole street like a bizarre Christmas tree.

Four

The junkie is better. He only has a few fractures. Enzo called, he tried to talk to Ekaterina, but she wasn't there. However, they told him that Bastiani is recovering from the accident.

Enzo is wearing the regulation dark-blue waterproof poncho, the brim of his cap sticking out from under the hood. He's explained everything to the police. It's clear that they will also have to talk to Sarti. Enzo has to speak to him too. That genius was in a big hurry, he told Enzo to let him know right away how his friend was, but he didn't leave a number. So now how is he supposed to get in touch with him?

A shitty night in any case, Lieutenant McClane. And all that rain that dripped into his pants before he remembered that he had the poncho isn't helping any either. But there's the patrol round to complete, the cards to slip under the doors. *It's a dirty job, but someone . . . Bullshit.* He could use some nice hot milk with brandy, Stravecchio, of course. That's for sure!

He gets in the car. Picks up the company phone.

"Central, do you read me?"

"Porretta, what is it?"

"We're done with the investigation here. I'm going to complete the rounds."

"Bravo."

"Anything new happening?"

"Italy is losing by one goal."

"Police news, I meant."

"Porretta . . ."

"Copy."

"Can you see okay?"

"Affirmative, Central, despite the heavy precipitation, the visual—"

"Then see that you go to h—"

End of conversation. He didn't catch the last part; the storm must have disrupted communications. *We're isolated, Lieutenant. We're on our own to face the night. All right then. We can do it! Die-hards, that's us.* He settles in, takes a towel from the duffel bag on the back seat, and dries off as best he can. There's still a piece of the Supremo and a few home fries left. A nice little bite was just what he needed. As he sinks his teeth into the sausage, christening the poncho with the first smear of mayonnaise accompanied by an inevitable "what the fuck," he starts the agency car and resumes his rounds.

He'll start with the street where the real-estate guy lives, the one who knows Sarti and asked for two security checks for him. Maybe that's where the out-of-towner went.

With this rain, you can't see a thing. He should revise his last exchange with Central, about being able to see well, but his sixth sense tells him that he'd better leave it alone. He drives slowly, almost at a crawl. And every time he has to get out to leave a card, an icy shower awaits. Tonight he'll be gobbling aspirin like Tic Tacs.

He turns into Germano's street, drives up to where it's blocked at the refinery plant, and pulls over to the curb to get out and drop off the cards.

But isn't that the guy's car? Sarti, the one who drove off in such a hurry? *Intuition is not something they hand out along with the uniform, Lieutenant.* Intuition is something you either have or don't have. And if you don't have it, you'd better leave it to others to do this work.

He gets out. Yeah, that's the car. No doubt about it. A nice toy. The very one he took off in to do some important thing the junkie told him to do.

Enzo gets back in the agency car and polishes off the Supremo accompanied by the spicy home fries, crispy earlier and now limp and soggy. He slips the third episode of *Die Hard*, the one with the bombs, into the DVD player. *I'll give him fifteen minutes, that Sarti, then I'll move on.*

It only takes ten.

There he is, that's him. He's coming out of the house where Germano lives, the agency guy who so firmly insisted that he monitor the house on Via delle Ortiche, because they were concerned there might be a thief casing the joint and instead it was that junkie. A lot of strange things are going on here tonight. Sarti seems like he's in a trance. He's walking in the rain, absolutely drenched, but he doesn't seem to care. Subject identified, in any case: now he has to make contact with him.

Enzo gets out of the car.

He approaches, about to say something.

It takes an instant.

Suddenly two headlights spring out of the darkness.

You know what marks the difference between people like us and people like them, Lieutenant? It's solely a matter of reflexes. That's it. None of that crap about the spirit of sacrifice or goodness of heart, that's just for bedtime stories. No, it's all about reflexes, and reflexes leave you no choice; they're triggered before you can ask any questions. You're like an animal, a panther that leaps in response to instinct. It's a heightened perception, as only some insects and certain ninja warriors have. A fucking war machine, that's what. Reflexes, either you have them or you don't. And if you don't have them, you'd better leave this work to others. Am I right, Lieutenant?

And with that he rushes forward.

Five

Sandro is lying on a gurney. He spent all night parked in a hospital corridor, because the ER was full. He's still there, lying under a blanket with a pattern of smiling teddy bears.

He's thinking.

As he explained to the policeman just a few minutes ago, he had forgotten to put the car in reverse and the vehicle had practically run over him because the hand brake doesn't hold. What had he gone there to do? He was high. Someone with all that heroin in his body does things that don't make much sense, right? But he sure wasn't driving. He doesn't see how you can call it a road accident. He's certainly no lawyer, but suspending his license seems unwarranted. He was on foot. He was walking after all. In fact, if he were the cop he would do a few . . . What do you call them? A few tests to *verify* that the damn hand brake works, because these American cars . . . you know how they are, maybe with a German car, it wouldn't have happened.

But apart from the version he gave to avoid telling the whole story about the telephone and Enrico, there is something else that he hasn't yet told them. There's that face that he could swear he saw inside the car. At first he couldn't place it. Then he recognized the blue cap, the clown hair sticking out at the sides. That pasty face and those vacant eyes. And he thinks he read it on his lips, in that split second artificially drawn-out by the drug: "Sandro, will you throw me the ball?" But he decided to deal with this aspect of the story on his own.

"You tried to kill me, you dirty son of a bitch. You finally decided to try it. But you know what? I think that at this point it's time we got some things clear. The reality that maybe you still don't get, you little shit, is that I would do it again. The only thing that drove me out of my mind was having let someone else take the blame. You can keep busting my balls every time I shoot up, you can pop up on the TV or even out of the toilet, but always be sure of one thing: that I would do it again. If only I could go back and save her, but I can't. So that's that. I'll expect you at the next hallucination. But I wanted to tell you that. I'm not afraid. No guilty feelings. To hell with you."

"Excuse me, what did you say?" The blonde girl with the Eastern European accent who was in the ambulance walks past him.

"I was thinking aloud."

"You were fortunate, you know?"

"Not that fortunate, let me tell you."

The girl smiles.

"Do you need anything?"

"I don't think so. On second thought, could I possibly get an ACE juice?"

Six

"Naturally the Evil Sisters had something to say about the olives, because, of course, they didn't like them. First they arrived early, and then they carped about everything, but 'not to criticize, Giulia dear, just saying.' It's my fault for wasting my time planning these evenings for them when they would be better off at a pizzeria. Yes, damn it, that's what I said. A pizzeria. Just think, when they served the shells with curried rice, Jessica was sure that curry was a plant. I mean really, doesn't she know that it's a *blend* of spices? Enrico? You know that at a certain point . . ."

Enrico is driving. He's been away a couple of days. After everything that happened he felt the need to go somewhere. When he returned, he stopped by the agency, signed the documents with Carmen, and is now on his way back to Rome. Before leaving town, he received a text from Betti.

We're burying Mom tomorrow. I don't think you'll come. As for all the rest, I know you've already decided. I would have liked to thank you. But it's all right this way. Love, B.

He did not reply.

That nutty guy had saved his life the other night, the guy who'd buzzed him on the intercom to tell him that Sandro was lying on the ground in front of his gate. Jumping out of nowhere in an instant, he'd rushed him and knocked him out of Steely Gloria's path. She had tried to kill him, and if the security guard hadn't been there, she very well would have succeeded. When they got up, Enrico still couldn't believe what had happened. He stood there staring at the Alfa while the security guard recited a whole speech about a sixth sense that only some insects and certain ninja warriors have.

The police arrived and went to Maurizio and Betti's house. While they were still inside, the living room curtain parted, and he saw Chiara. She'd looked at him, raised her hand, and waved. Enrico did the same. For a moment, he'd thought of saying something, to her or to Betti. But he had no idea what to say. He got in the car, drove past the house, slowed, but did not stop. He continued on at a crawl until he came to the end of the street. He turned down another street, and drove until he reached the Aurelia, still moving very slowly. One direction led to Rome. He went the other way.

And kept on going. He turned on the stereo, found something decent, and turned up the volume. He didn't know the car had such a great stereo. And he went on driving. Nothing but earsplitting music and the road to keep him company. For kilometers and kilometers. He stopped at an Autogrill, bought all the U2 CDs he could find, and set out again. He drove some more, until the night came to an end. And still he kept on driving. He drove on, as the sky grew lighter and the sun rose. Then farther still, crossing the border into France. Nice, Cannes, Marseille, Provence, Languedoc. He continued on, reading the names on the road signs, surprised at how close those places he'd never been were. He went on driving, losing all sense of time, through Aquitaine, as far as Biarritz. And there he finally stopped.

He reached for the hand brake, then, not finding it, he remembered the button. He got out and looked for a bar. He found one, ordered a coffee, and stood gazing at the ocean for what felt like an eternity.

It's windy. No whaling ships, but he saw surfers in wetsuits chal-lenging the huge waves of the Atlantic.

Alice was right. It didn't take all that long to get there. And being there, in front of the ocean, at this moment, is actually enough. Reason enough to have come.

He goes down to the beach. Walks along the shore. Looks at the sea. In his pocket is Alice's phone. That tiny memory card contains a truth that has been buried for ten years. A secret in which the lives of all of them have remained trapped. It's time to set them free.

"You don't want to throw it into the sea," Alice says, who is there walking beside him now, on the beach in Biarritz.

"Why not?"

"Because that stuff pollutes."

"Does that seem like something to say at a time like this?"

Alice moves closer.

"You're really going to do it?"

"Wouldn't it be nice to throw it out there? And stand here watching as it vanishes in the waves?"

"As long as it's the first and last time."

"I promise. I won't toss any more old cell phones into the ocean."

He pulls up her last message on the display.

He sees that half an hour has passed.

He turns off the phone. Brings it to his lips. One more breath. And off it goes.

It's a long throw. The phone's arc in the sky is a hushed rainbow.

Then it hits the water and sinks. And, in a few seconds, everything that was in its memory no longer exists.

Enrico continues gazing at the waves for a while longer. The smell of sea salt is stronger here.

He turns, walks to the car. And heads back.

The return trip always seems shorter. It makes no sense, since the distance is the same. But it's the mind and soul of the one traveling it that are different. And it's proof that space and time change, depending on what you carry inside you.

Soon after he crosses the border, he stops at an Autogrill. He's famished and returns to the car with a bag full of tuna sandwiches. He sleeps a few hours in a rest area along the highway, where he meets Costantin, a gigantic truck driver, who each day drives more or less the same distance that he has just covered, and who can't understand how anyone could find any pleasure in doing that, for no reason, just for the sake of driving, unless someone paid him to do it. Costantin has a thermos of coffee that his girlfriend, Irene, always makes for him. No one knows how to make coffee the way she does. He offers Enrico a cup and listens intently as he tells him about his drive. About having stopped to watch the ocean. About how vast and deep the Eastern Sea is and about the frog who becomes sad when the tortoise shows her how small her pond is by comparison. Maybe Costantin doesn't fully understand it all, maybe it will take him ten years to understand, as it took Enrico. The truck driver shows him the photo of Irene that he keeps on the dashboard. He tells him that they don't see each other very much and that he knows exactly where he would go, only he can't do it. They piss together behind a bush. Then they leave, each going his separate way.

Giulia's call came a few minutes before he got on the ring road.

". . . Well anyway, the Evil Sisters never change. But where on earth are you? When did you say you'd be back? Because, if you like, I'll let you taste the baby octopus soup, with the olives, then you can give me your take on it. And tell me about how it went, okay? I want to hear all about your friends. Better yet, why don't we invite them here to our place some day? As soon as we're settled in the new apartment, we could plan a dinner with them. What do you think? Oh, and I thought of something else, but this is really fabulous, so get comfortable and I'll tell you about it. Do you remember that house in the mountains, in Canazei? Well, the other day this guy called me . . ."

Seven

There are a people who live in Peru, on the high plateau of Lake Titicaca, the Aymara. They are convinced that the future lies behind us. That we all walk backward in life, and that what we see in front of us is our past. To say that something has yet to happen, the Aymara point behind them. And to say that something has happened, they point ahead of them. All in all, I think it is a way to understand the value of what you've done, of what you've come to know. How important it is to safeguard it as best you can, always keep it there, before you, as it should be, because it's all you have. And walking backward, step by step, your field of vision widens and you get the impression that you can see things better, understand them.

That morning I woke up early. Outside the reddish tint of dawn still lingered on the trees. I had a few things to do, but it was so early that I rolled up the shutter and stayed in bed, staring out. And it was "one of those moments," as I called them.

It happens sometimes. It's as if at some point, everything was composed to perfection, like an orchestra in which everyone is playing a different melody that only at that instant, unexpectedly, becomes the same melody. And it's never planned or anticipated, like birthdays or holidays, not like Christmas morning or New Year's Eve or the night of San Lorenzo. No, at first glance, they are always insignificant. But then it seems like something hits you, and you are in that moment. Everything is suddenly in its rightful place, and you feel like you could stay there forever. And I think even dear old William Blake knew this feeling when he wrote to "Hold Infinity in the palm of your hand / And Eternity in an hour."

I don't know why, but in the end, you realize that going there is worth a lifetime.

And from the smile that instantly appears on Chiara's lips as she sits in her usual bus shelter waiting for the bus to school, backpack resting on the ground between her legs, and earbuds carrying Chris's voice directly into her soul, it's all too easy to see that this, for her, is "one of those moments."

The old posters have been replaced, and now there's one for a yoga center. This year Chiara is taking her final graduation exams. She has some ideas about what to do afterward, but the fact that it is still completely open is a privilege that I hope she can take her time to consider. Meanwhile, she's about to leave for London, to spend the summer with Margherita. A year has passed since the night Gloria died. At first it seemed impossible to live with *that thing*. Then the days went by, as they always do, and *that thing* grew fainter, and it faded away. It happens like that, a situation that at first you think will crush you, you realize one day that you haven't thought about it for a while and you know you'll survive. Chiara has already bought a suitcase so big that she herself could fit into it. For now, it's in her room, standing on the floor. There's still some time before the trip, but she likes to see it waiting there, right under the poster of *Into the Wild*.

The house is quiet now. There's nobody home. The kitchen is spotless. The cup with the roses that her mother uses for her morning green tea is turned over by the sink. In the plate, next to the front door, her father has forgotten his orange lighter. The almond tree in their garden is in bloom, covered in a blanket of white flowers. Among the many things that no one around here will ever know about is the rock that lies at the foot of that tree.

It's a big rock. There are similar ones around it, but a certain detail would not escape a sharp eye. It is precisely the one: the rock with which I was killed. Gloria left it there, without telling anyone. Maybe she dumped it, planning to get rid of it later. Then she must have thought: What better place than the backyard to hide something like that? I can just hear her, that crazy old woman, saying that certain things mustn't leave the family. And no one has ever known. No one ever noticed it, during suppers served al fresco, afternoons spent outside reading and watching the world go by, Chiara's birthdays with cake and candles, summer evenings spent enjoying the cool air, all the life that takes place in a normal backyard, and that has slipped away, in the company of that rock.

No one spotted it, just as no one ever noticed the moth that at times, in the dead of night, comes to rest right there on top of it. It flits around the tree a little. It dances in the light of the small lamp fixture next to the gate. It flutters down, gliding gently, until it comes to settle on that very rock. Sometimes it waits for the kitchen window to open, so it can fly inside and linger in the house a while. When you know the story, you can't help but stop and think about it. After all, they say strange things about moths. About how they sometimes enter houses. Old superstitions, popular beliefs. There are few people left, these days, who are familiar with them.

ABOUT THE AUTHOR

Riccardo Bruni is an Italian journalist who writes for newspapers, magazines, webzines, and blogs. *The Night of the Moths* is his second novel translated into English, following *The Lion and the Rose*. *La stagione del biancospino* (*The Hawthorne Season*) will be his next translated work. He is also the author of the novels *La lunga notte dell'Iguana*, *Nessun dolore*, and *Zona d'ombra*. For more information, please visit www.riccardobruni.com.

ABOUT THE TRANSLATOR

Anne Milano Appel, PhD, was awarded the Italian Prose in Translation Award (2015), the John Florio Prize for Italian Translation (2013), and the Northern California Book Award for Translation—Fiction (2014, 2013). She has translated works by Claudio Magris, Primo Levi, Giovanni Arpino, Paolo Giordano, Roberto Saviano, Giuseppe Catozzella, and numerous others. Translating professionally since 1996, she is a former library director and language teacher, with a BA in Art and English Literature (UCLA), an MLS in Library Services (Rutgers), and an MA and PhD in Romance Languages (Rutgers).